PLYMOUTH UNDERCOVER

PAMELA KELLEY

PIPING PLOVER PRESS, INC.

INTRODUCTION

Meet Emma McCarthy, a thirty-year-old failed actress that just moved home to Plymouth, MA.

And her mother, Cindy, a yoga instructor in the Pinehills, an exclusive golf community in Plymouth.

They've just inherited Court Street Investigations, a private detective agency.

And its one part-time employee, eighty-year-old Mickey, a retired police detective.

They expect typical cases like cheating spouses or workman's comp, but quickly learn that the agency also has a reputation for solving murders.

CHAPTER 1

"You're really going to give up on acting? To be a private investigator? I think you might be having a mid-life crisis," Emma's soon-to-be-former roommate, said.

They'd been friends since meeting freshman year in the film program at UCLA. Emma's dream had been acting, and she'd moved to L.A. right after high school and spent a year waitressing and establishing residency so she could get the in-state rate for tuition.

Lexy's focus was on film production, specifically directing, and she was well on her way. She'd been working as a production assistant for various shows and just landed a new role with ShondaLand, a woman-owned company with several hot series at Netflix, and Emma was thrilled for her.

"I just turned thirty a month ago. It's been almost ten years since I graduated from college and it hasn't happened for me. It would have by now." Emma had come to terms with her decision. She was at peace with it after losing her father two months ago. When she'd headed back east for the funeral, to her hometown of Plymouth, MA, she'd felt a surprising pull to return.

When she'd moved to L.A. after high school, she couldn't wait for her life to begin and to get as far away from Plymouth as possible. It wasn't that she didn't like her hometown. Even though it was the state's biggest town geographically, it still felt like a small town, as she couldn't go anywhere without running into someone she knew. But all she'd ever wanted to do was to be an actress, and that wasn't going to happen in Plymouth.

So, she went to UCLA, which had one of the best film programs. And she'd been so hopeful for so long. She'd gotten the occasional bit part and finally what she thought was her big break, as part of an ensemble cast for a sitcom. But it never got picked up, and the feedback from those who saw it was that she really wasn't very funny, so maybe she should stick to dramas. Which she happily would have done, if they'd given her a chance. But no one ever did. The competition for acting roles was more fierce than Emma had ever imagined.

She'd always felt reasonably attractive. She was short at barely five two, but she ran and did yoga to stay a size four—that was important as the camera added a good ten to fifteen pounds. Her hair was a deep chestnut brown—long and naturally wavy, it was her best feature.

Her nose was maybe a little bigger than average, which probably immediately took her off many lists, as everyone in Hollywood seemed to have perfect noses—

small, sculpted and rarely original. But Emma never considered surgery. Well, she did once, and then came to her senses. She had her dad's nose and it fit her face.

She also knew that many surgeries had complications, with collapsed valves and breathing issues, and she didn't need that. But still, the reality was that she was up against other prettier, thinner, more talented or more connected actresses and she was tired of losing out to them. She was tired of all of it.

She looked around the tiny apartment in the Hollywood Hills that she'd shared with Lexy. For what Emma paid for her share of the rent, she could rent a cottage on White Horse Beach all to herself. And she did—before she flew back to L.A., she signed a lease on an adorable place.

Her mother called it a beach shack, and Emma supposed she was right. It was one of many small cottages that literally sat on the sand at White Horse Beach. Most of them were only used in the summer. But a few, like Emma's, were year-round.

It was tiny, just a little over six hundred square feet, but it was ocean front, with a deck almost as big as the cottage. It had a small kitchen, one bedroom and bathroom, and a cozy living room with big windows looking out at the ocean.

She was lucky to get it. Most of those cottages were strictly summer rentals, as the owners could charge crazy high weekly prices because of the location. The owner, Helen Whitman, was an older woman who had been a client of her father's. She'd said that she didn't want to deal with weekly rentals anymore, and was tired of worrying about cleaning it every Saturday before the next arrival.

Emma also suspected she'd had a soft spot for her father, and maybe they'd chatted about Emma moving home if anything happened to him. Because when her father's attorney read the will to them, there was a note for Emma to call Helen for a possible lead on a rental.

Emma's mother had suggested her house in the Pine-hills, which had plenty of room. But moving home to Plymouth and back in with her mother was a step further than Emma wanted to go. The beach cottage was perfect, and she knew her mother understood.

"Maybe I am having a bit of a mid-life crisis," Emma admitted. "I just feel like I should be further ahead than I am at age thirty. It's one of those numbers that makes you stop and evaluate where you are and where you want to be. You know?"

Lexy nodded. "I do. I get it. For what it's worth, I think you're enormously talented and maybe if you stayed, someone might figure that out, eventually."

"Maybe. But maybe not." Emma smiled. "I can always act in local theater productions."

"You could. Private investigating, though. Are you sure you want to do that?"

"Reasonably sure. Enough to give it a good shot. When I was in high school, I used to help my father in the office. He always told me I was a natural. I answered his phones and did some basic research for him on the internet."

Emma smiled at the memory of it. She'd loved working with him. Once she moved out to California, she hadn't given it another thought though, until recently. It was going to be strange to be in his office without him, but it felt like it was something she needed to try.

"He left it to you and your mother to run together? Why not your brother too? I would think that kind of thing would be more up a guy's alley?" Lexy asked.

"Matt never had any interest in it. He's also crazy busy with his car repair business."

Her older brother and his best friend, Ryan, owned a business together, repairing cars and storing them in the winter. Business was booming and Emma was proud of him. He was doing what he loved.

"How's your mother doing with it? Didn't she used to help your dad too?"

"She did some, before they divorced. She mostly ran the office part-time for him while he was out in the field. It's been a long time though, and I think she's feeling a little overwhelmed. And it's a lot for Mickey to handle on his own."

"Who's Mickey?"

"My dad's employee. He's wonderful—an older retired detective that mostly works part time for something to do. My mom has had him working full time the past few weeks, and she's worried that she might be burning him out."

Lexy sighed. "So, it sounds like they need you. Do I have to worry about you? Is this kind of work dangerous?"

Emma laughed. "No. It's nothing like you see on TV. It's a lot of driving around, sitting and waiting, or surfing the internet trying to track people down. It's actually kind of fun. And we're always careful. We have to be, so we aren't spotted following someone."

"That's not exactly reassuring. Stay safe and call me once you get settled. I'm going to miss you." Lexy's voice cracked a little.

Emma felt her eyes water. She was going to miss her life in L.A. and especially Lexy, too.

"I will. You'll probably get sick of hearing from me."

"WHY DON'T YOU JUST SELL THE BUSINESS? YOU HAVEN'T worked in Fred's office in over twenty years. Is this really what you want to do?" Cindy's best friend, Rachel, asked.

They were all sitting on their other best friend, Lee's, back deck. It was Friday night, a little after six thirty, which meant happy hour. They lived a few houses apart on a cul de sac in the Pinehills, a golf community in Plymouth. None of them golfed, though their husbands had.

Lee's house was in the middle and had the best deck, so that's usually where they went. Cindy brought the Bread and Butter chardonnay, Rachel brought the pub cheese and crackers, and Lee had some frozen pizzas heating up in the oven and sipped a vodka and soda because she hated wine. The three of them had been friends for close to thirty years, since they'd all been newly married and moved into the neighborhood.

Lee was the only one of the three that was still married. Her husband, Bob, was a great guy who was semi-retired and was happiest down in his basement, doing his woodworking projects or golfing with his buddies. Rachel was widowed about five years ago and Cindy had been divorced for almost twenty years now. Though with Fred's recent passing, she felt a bit like a widow too, especially as he'd left his private investigating agency equally to her and her daughter, Emma.

It hadn't surprised Cindy that he'd left the business to Emma as she'd always been good at it, and she guessed it was Fred's way of tempting Emma to move home, to be closer to her family. Cindy was surprised that he'd included her too, though.

Cindy had worked at the agency with Fred when they were married, but it was just to help out. She'd never shared the passion for the business that Fred and Emma had. But maybe he'd also thought it would be good for both of them.

She really didn't know what had gone through Fred's mind. He hadn't shared any of it with her. He hadn't even told them he was sick until he only had a month left. He'd had a rare brain cancer that had been discovered at a late stage, and there wasn't really anything they could do. The only blessing was that he said he'd felt good until he didn't and then passed a few weeks later. It was still a shock she was trying to get used to.

She hadn't seen Fred much in recent years, but when

they did bump into each other, it was always civil, much like seeing an old friend. Their divorce had been amicable too, as far as a divorce could be. There was, of course, plenty of sadness and disappointment on both sides, but there was no anger. The relationship just hadn't worked out.

Fred had gone on to have several long-term relationships and Cindy had dated here and there, but it never turned into anything serious. And after a while, she just stopped trying. It was easier to put off trying to find someone else than to 'get out there' as Rachel often said. Rachel had ventured into online dating a few years ago and kept them entertained with her various dating disasters. She still kept at it, though, while Cindy held off.

Though Fred's passing was a wake-up call. In the blink of an eye, twenty years had passed and Cindy was still alone. She told herself she liked it that way, but truth be told, she envied what Lee and Bob had, their companionship. Maybe she should make more of an effort. The thought of online dating, like what Rachel was doing, was intimidating though. It was easier to put it off and hope that maybe she'd just bump into someone somewhere, the way it used to happen when she was younger.

She turned her attention back to Rachel's question. "We can't sell it. Fred was the business. Without him, there's nothing to buy."

"Oh. Hmm. Well, maybe once Emma gets here it might be fun for you?" Rachel said.

"It's not too much for you?" Lee asked.

Cindy shook her head. "I thought it might be, but it's

really not. Most of my yoga classes are early evening and a few mornings. The other girls handle the mid-day and weekend classes. And I hired a new girl last week to take over a few of my classes to free up more time."

Cindy started the yoga studio years ago, while she was still married and the business had grown over the years. She'd always loved yoga, how it quieted her mind, helped ease any stiffness or achy muscles and kept her in shape. And she had a great group of regular customers that had become friends over the years.

"Thank goodness for Mickey though. I don't know what I'd do without him. I've never done any of the actual investigative work, like surveillance. He's been busy these past few weeks," Cindy said.

"How old is he?" Lee asked.

"I think he's almost eighty. But he's sharp as a tack and in good shape. Except for the donut eating. He needs to cut back on that, but he says it goes along with surveillance work."

Rachel laughed. "Sounds like an excuse to eat donuts to me."

Cindy nodded. "He said his wife, Betty, read him the riot act recently. She watches his diet pretty closely." Mickey was a character. She knew he missed police work and enjoyed keeping busy.

"Speaking of age, what are we going to do for Rachel's birthday? It's a big one," Lee said.

"Double-nickels!" Cindy said and then laughed. Mickey had teased her a few weeks ago when she'd turned fifty-five and had said her double-nickels birthday was good luck. "How about 42 for stuffed lobsters?" The nearby restaurant, 42 Degrees North, had the best stuffed lobsters in the area. Occasionally they went there and splurged.

Rachel nodded. "That sounds perfect to me. I think I deserve a baked stuffed lobster." She glanced at Lee and Cindy. "I think we all do."

CHAPTER 2

Emma loved looking out the window whenever she flew into Boston's Logan Airport. As they flew over the city, she could see the streets of downtown Boston below and they looked like such a tangle. Unlike most modern cities with their carefully planned growth and perfect grid of streets, Boston was a bit of a mess with one-ways and streets that didn't go where you would expect. But as they drew closer and she could see Boston Harbor below, she felt a thrill. She was almost home. It felt like a new beginning and, although she was sad to give up on her dream, she was looking forward to settling into her beach cottage and starting work at the agency.

When she got off the plane, she collected her two giant suitcases and made her way to a shuttle to the rental car agency. Eventually, she settled into her rental car, a silver Honda CRV and two hours later, after getting stuck in some rush hour traffic going through the city, she arrived at her rental at White Horse Beach. She grabbed the bigger of the two suitcases and dragged it down the wooden walkway and through the beach grass and sand until she reached the back door. The key was under the mat, as Helen had said it would be. Emma unlocked the door, shoved her suitcase inside and went back for the other one.

Once her luggage was in, she put it in the bedroom and went out on the front deck and took a deep breath of the fresh, salt air. She'd gotten used to the smog of L.A. and this was so much better. It was late April, and the sun was shining brightly, but the air was cool. Emma knew it would take her a while to get used to the difference in temperature. L.A. was much warmer this time of year.

Even in April though, at almost five o'clock, there were still people out walking along the beach. White Horse Beach was a little over a mile long, a white, sandy beach lined with cottages and the occasional larger home. The water was shallow, but in recent years it had become a favorite hunting ground for great white sharks. They liked to feed off the seals that sunned themselves on the rocks.

Emma remembered her mother telling her that two summers ago there had been a scare when two college girls in kayaks had foolishly paddled out to the jetty where the seals liked to sunbathe. A shark had attacked one of the kayaks, testing to see if it was a seal. Both boats capsized and fortunately the shark swam away, disappointed when it realized the kayak wasn't a seal.

The girls were very lucky that the shark wasn't interested in them and that they were quickly rescued by the coast guard. When asked why they'd gone to such a dangerous area where sharks were known to visit, one of them had said, "We heard a shark had eaten a seal earlier that day, so we didn't think it would still be hungry."

So, tempted as she was to try paddle boarding, Emma decided to stick to the lakes for that and just get her feet wet in the ocean instead. She was excited to get up early and have her coffee on the deck in the morning and watch the sunrise. Reluctantly, she went back inside. She didn't have time to stay on the beach and daydream. She and her brother, Matt, were expected at their mother's house for dinner—a welcome home dinner for Emma. She just about had time to put some of her clothes away and take a quick shower before heading over to the Pinehills.

CINDY FUSSED AROUND THE KITCHEN, CHECKING THE TIME before putting a tray of her famous cheesy artichoke garlic bread in the oven. The kids loved that. She mixed chopped artichokes with garlic, butter, sour cream and two different kinds of cheeses, then slathered it on both halves of a loaf of Italian bread and baked it until bubbly. She also made a tossed garden salad to go with Emma's favorite meal, chicken, broccoli and ziti with Alfredo sauce. It wasn't a low cal meal, but now and then Cindy liked to indulge, especially if she was cooking for others.

Her oldest child, Matt, was the first to arrive with his girlfriend, Dana. Matt recently turned thirty-three, and Dana was the same age. She was an elementary school teacher, and Cindy really liked her for Matt. They balanced each other out. Dana was calm and relaxing while Matt was high energy and outgoing. They weren't engaged yet, but Cindy had a feeling it might be coming soon, and she approved.

Matt gave his mother a big hug and kiss on the cheek, and Dana did the same. He put a six-pack of beer in the refrigerator and handed Cindy a chilled bottle of wine. "This is the one you like, right? Butter?"

Cindy smiled. "This is great, thanks honey." Bread and Butter was actually her favorite, but Butter was good too.

Cindy opened the wine and poured a glass for herself and Dana while Matt grabbed one of the beers that he'd brought. A moment later, she heard a car pull in the driveway. Emma walked through the door with a bottle of wine as well, Bread and Butter, which Cindy thanked her for and put in the refrigerator to keep cool. Emma helped herself to a glass of wine and they went on Cindy's back deck to relax before dinner.

Emma caught them up on her final days in California and told them about the cottage.

"You all have to come over soon to see it. It's small, but it's going to be great this summer. I'll have a third of July party on the deck—it's the same size as the house!"

"That will be fun, honey. I haven't been over to White

Horse Beach on the third in years." Unlike the rest of the country, White Horse Beach held its Fourth of July celebration on the third. It was a tradition that started many years ago and it was like a giant neighborhood block party.

Taylor Avenue, the main road that along the beach, shut down, and the police patrolled the area to make sure no one got out of hand. Oddly enough, although fireworks were illegal in Massachusetts, there was an understanding of some sort and the police allowed it to happen on the third. Along with bonfires up and down the beach. The fireworks were often more spectacular than the official town fireworks the following day.

They headed back inside for dinner and for the next two hours, Cindy was pretty much in heaven. It was such a treat to have both of her children under the same roof. She felt bad for Emma that her dream of being an actress hadn't gone the way she'd hoped. But Cindy was glad that her daughter was back in Plymouth and she hoped that she'd be happy working at the agency.

Fred had always thought that Emma had a talent for it. She had always done well in school, especially in math. She loved to solve puzzles and was always curious about how things worked. Cindy was more than happy to hand over the computer work to Emma and she'd focus on the office management duties, accounting and that kind of thing.

"So, what time do you want me at the office tomorrow?" Emma asked over coffee. She'd refused dessert, which didn't surprise Cindy. Matt and Dana happily said yes to cheesecake though, and Cindy indulged in a small slice as well. She got up and opened a desk drawer in the kitchen and returned with a set of keys for Emma.

"I usually go in around nine, but here's your keys for the front and back doors. Mickey usually comes in around ten."

"Okay, I'll probably shoot for eight thirty or so, to get settled and have another cup of coffee. Do we have much going on right now?"

"Mickey has a surveillance job in Kingston tomorrow. That's really it. We were crazy busy the past two weeks but closed out a few cases and it's slowing down some."

Emma laughed. "Figures, now that I'm here. Maybe I'll go along with Mickey and keep him company. I've never gone on surveillance. Dad would never let me."

"I suppose that would be okay." Cindy felt a bit unsure, but realized it was ridiculous. If they were sending a man out who was almost eighty, then of course it was safe for her thirty-year-old daughter to go.

"Mom, I'm going to have to learn how to do it. We can't rely on Mickey totally for that kind of stuff."

Cindy nodded. "I know. I know. I'm still getting used to being back in that world again."

"If you ever get stuck or want someone to go with you… I'm happy to help," Matt offered.

"I don't want to take you away from your work, honey," Cindy said.

"Thanks, Matt. Hopefully we won't need to take you up on that, but I appreciate the offer," Emma said.

"Between Emma and Mickey, we should be able to handle things. We don't generally get very exciting cases," Cindy said.

"What are most of your cases like?" Dana asked.

"The bread and butter cases are often surveillance for people who suspect their spouse is being unfaithful. Sometimes it's finding someone that has disappeared owing money and we track them down. Occasionally we work with law firms or insurance companies—particularly workman's comp claims and we find evidence that they are not injured as they claim."

"Those are the most interesting," Emma said.

"Speaking of interesting. Did you hear that local woman is still missing?" Matt said.

"What woman?" Emma asked.

"Nancy Eldridge. She was a new partner at the biggest law firm in Plymouth and young too, in her late thirties. She went out to dinner with friends a few weeks ago, went home and no one has seen her since," Cindy said.

"That's so sad," Dana said.

"They haven't turned up anything useful yet," Cindy said. "I just read about it this morning. Scary thing is, it looks like she made it home and someone was waiting for her in her garage. There was pepper spray residue on the garage door."

"That doesn't sound good," Emma said.

"No, it's awful. Fortunately, we don't get cases like that." She glanced at Emma. "Tomorrow will be a good day for you to go out with Mickey. It's a pretty straightforward case. The wife suspects that her husband is seeing someone else, either on his lunch hour or right after work. She doesn't believe he's just working late so often."

Emma smiled. "We'll find out."

CHAPTER 3

After eating all that pasta and garlic bread, Emma was home and in bed by a little before nine. All the traveling had caught up with her and even with the three-hour time difference, she still fell fast asleep and woke up the next morning at seven sharp feeling refreshed and ready to start the day. She made herself a cup of black coffee from the tiny, single-serving Keurig machine in the compact kitchen, and took it outside, grabbing a sweatshirt along the way.

The air was cool, and the sweatshirt was necessary, but the hot coffee kept her warm and the sun was already shining over the ocean. The skies were clear and blue with swirling cotton candy clouds. It was going to be a beautiful day. Emma was excited for her first day on the job and to go on surveillance with Mickey. He'd been working with her father for as long as she could remember, and she'd always adored him. Everyone did. He pretended to be gruff, but it was all an act. He was as soft as a marshmallow, and he was still razor sharp.

Her father often said Mickey had an eye for details, noticing the smallest things that her father didn't always catch. And Mickey had the patience for surveillance work. Emma knew from what her father had told her, that the majority of the time it could be pretty boring—lots of sitting and waiting for something to happen.

She sipped her coffee and watched the waves crashing on the beach. Even this early, there were people out walking, some with dogs racing ahead of them and darting into the water. Maybe later, at the end of the day, she'd take a walk along the beach herself. Or another morning, she could go before work. She normally was up a bit earlier, around six.

After a second cup of coffee and a browse of the local news on her phone, Emma jumped in the shower and got ready for her first day. She stopped at Dunkin' Donuts on her way to the office and grabbed a few everything bagels with cream cheese and a box of munchkins—the delicious donut holes—in case Mickey wanted a snack while they were waiting.

She arrived at the office at a quarter past eight and was the first one there. Her father had owned the office condo that was in an old brick building at the beginning of Main Street in downtown Plymouth. Technically, that end of Main Street was called Court Street, but everyone referred to it as Main Street. Plymouth was funny like that.

Their office was on the first floor and there was a

short flight of stairs to the front door. There was a small kitchen area, and Emma made herself another cup of coffee before sitting down at a desk that sat in front of a bay window that overlooked Main Street. The office had high ceilings and two fireplaces that looked nice, but as the building was over a hundred years old, they were strongly encouraged not to use them.

Even this early, there were people walking along Main Street. Plymouth was a historic tourist town, settled in 1620 and known for the Pilgrims, the Mayflower, and Plymouth Rock. Emma always warned people when they visited, and she took them to see the rock for the first time. Everyone always imagined it would be bigger. The Mayflower was less of a disappointment. It was an exact replica and sat proudly in Plymouth Harbor, open to all to visit and tour.

The office looked exactly as she remembered from the last time she'd visited her father. They'd had lunch plans, and she'd stopped in and said hello to Mickey before she and her father walked down to the waterfront for a leisurely lunch at East Bay Grille. Although they had an extensive menu, Emma almost always got the same thing —a lobster roll. Theirs was the best in Plymouth. It made her sad thinking of it now.

Even after the divorce, she and her father had been close, though she only saw him a few times a year, when she'd come home for the holidays. They'd talked often though, at least once a week, and Emma missed those weekly calls. More than once, when something good or bad had happened, she'd reached for the phone to call her dad and then remembered she couldn't do that anymore. She felt her eyes grow misty and took a deep breath. The sadness took her by surprise at times.

She'd talked to her mother about it and she'd assured her that it was normal and that the first year after someone passed was always the hardest, especially around any milestone dates, birthdays, holidays or anytime a memory was triggered.

Emma wondered if it was strange for her mother to be working back at the agency again. She was glad that she was, though. Emma's gift was not organization. She still struggled with paying bills on time, even when she had the money.

Emma turned on the computer and opened Outlook and the office calendar. She saw the schedule for the week; surveillance today on the Campbell case. Then Wednesday and Thursday it looked like they were booked for a workman's comp case.

There was a phone message and an email from a Belinda Russell asking that they please call her as soon as possible. Emma called and got voice mail. She left a message for Belinda to call back and left the main number, so her mother could take the call while they were out.

She took the last bite of her bagel as the front door opened and her mother walked in holding a paper cup of coffee from Kiskadee, a coffee shop on Main Street.

"Did you eat yet?" Emma asked. "I brought bagels and munchkins."

"I did, honey. That's nice of you, though. I'm sure Mickey will want some."

Once her mother got settled, she walked Emma through their current caseload, which at the moment, was just the two that were on the calendar already.

"Sydney Campbell's is the suspected infidelity case. She said her husband, Sean, has been distant lately and has been coming home from work later and later. He's also lost some weight and has started dressing better. All the usual red flags."

"What does he do for work?"

"It's a family-owned business in the industrial park. They make paper products, pizza boxes, takeout containers. Her husband started it with his two brothers years ago, and it sounds like it's doing very well. She said they doubled their revenue last year. That's another thing—she said they used to go on fancy vacations, but this year it's been work trips instead and he's gone by himself to multiple conferences."

"That doesn't sound good," Emma said.

"No, and he just bought an expensive new car, too. A flashy red Lamborghini."

"Maybe he's having a mid-life crisis?" Emma wondered.

Her mother laughed. "That's what I said too, and Sydney agrees. She said this all started when her husband turned fifty a year ago. But her gut is telling her he's having an affair. And if it's true, she's immediately going for a divorce."

"I hope it's not true. Maybe they can save their

marriage if it's just a mid-life crisis."

"Your father once said that eighty-five percent of the people that think their spouse is having an affair, are correct. So, the odds don't look good. But, that would be nice."

"So, where does she want us to start?"

"She said he's often hard to reach at lunchtime and right after work. He always tells her he was just busy working, but she wants us to find out for sure. So, you two will go to his company and wait to see if he goes anywhere during the day, most likely at lunchtime, and then see where he goes at the end of the day—if it's straight home, or elsewhere."

"Will do. Oh, a Belinda Russell called and emailed. I left her a message, so she may be calling you. She didn't say much in her message or email, so I'm not sure what she needs help with."

"I'll find out, if she calls in. And if you need anything, call me. I'll be here."

Until Mickey arrived, her mother walked her through the cases they'd handled in recent weeks. There was quite a variety, from similar ones dealing with infidelity, to personal injury or workman's comp cases for insurance companies to finding people that skipped out on rent.

At ten, Mickey arrived, looking like someone's favorite grandfather with a thick head of snowy white hair, twinkling blue eyes and a rosy nose and cheeks. He wore a Red Sox baseball hat and a Mr. Rogers style gray cardigan over a crisp white button-down shirt, and tan pants.

After they exchanged hellos, Mickey grabbed a set of binoculars off his desk.

"Are you ready to go, Emma?"

She jumped up and pulled on her windbreaker and slung her purse over her shoulders. "I'm ready."

When they walked outside and into the parking lot, Emma saw her mother's navy Audi sedan, her father's silver Honda, which Emma was now using, and an adorable baby blue convertible.

"Is that your car, Mickey? What is it?"

"A Chrysler Crossfire. Has a Mercedes engine, you know. That thing can fly." He smiled. "I get a lot of attention in that car. You should probably drive."

Emma laughed. "Yes, we'll take my car."

He nodded. "Your mother used to let me take hers. Sometimes I drive our other car, a silver Toyota Corolla. But it's so nice out today that I had to take the convertible."

They climbed into Emma's Honda and she handed Mickey the Dunkin' Donuts bag. "There's a bagel and cream cheese in there or donuts, if you'd rather."

"Well, aren't you thoughtful?" He opened the bag and took a peek inside. "Oh, munchkins are my favorite. They're so small it's like I'm not being bad at all."

Emma laughed as she plugged the address into her GPS. She knew the area they were going to. Thirty-seven Resnik Road was just off Industrial Park Road near the Registry of Motor Vehicles.

It took them a little over ten minutes to get to the office park and to Plymouth Paper Company. She knew from the quick research she'd done in the office, that the company employed about fifty people and there were about that many cars in the parking lot. They found a spot with a view of the front door and turned off the engine.

"And now we wait," Mickey said. He popped another munchkin in his mouth while Emma searched the internet on her phone to see what else she could find on Sean Campbell. She found his Facebook page and it had a good recent picture of him.

Sydney had emailed one to her mother as well, but it wasn't as good as this one. The Facebook one was dated a week ago, and he was all dressed up for a night out, in a black suit and red power tie. His black hair was tinged with gray around the edges and slicked back with gel. He wasn't a bad-looking guy for his age. Emma had never been one to go for older men, but she knew women her age in L.A. that would find Sean, his flashiness and his money, quite attractive.

"What was it like, being a detective? Do you miss it?" Emma asked Mickey.

He smiled. "I liked it, most of the time. And sometimes, I miss it. But, not usually. I don't miss the politics of it, that's for sure."

"How long have you worked for my dad?"

"Let's see. I turn eighty in two months and that will be twenty years. That's something, isn't it?"

"That's impressive. Do you think you'll want to keep working?" Emma hoped so, but couldn't blame Mickey if he was ready to call it quits.

He laughed. "As long as you'll have me, I'll stay with it. What else would I do? I like to keep busy and as my wife says, it keeps me out of trouble."

"This is probably safer than being a detective, I would think?"

"Yes. And I'm smart about it." He was quiet for a moment before saying, "Your father wasn't always as cautious. He was fearless, but I told him sometimes that he was foolish too. He took unnecessary risks. Stick with me, kid, and I'll show you the smart, safe way to do this job."

Emma wasn't surprised to hear it. She knew her father was often impulsive and overly enthusiastic, which sometimes led to being careless. He'd never gotten himself into trouble, but from some of his stories, she'd suspected that he'd come close a few times.

"Smart and safe sounds good to me." Emma continued scrolling through Sean's Facebook page. He liked to post pictures of himself and his toys. She saw the fancy car. It was pretty, she had to admit. She groaned at the image of Sean holding two heavy weights, and with no shirt on. He did seem to be in good shape, but the no shirt, gym tan and thick gold chains around his neck made her cringe. But, from all the comments on the picture, many of them from women, she in the minority.

Mickey told her stories of his detective days as they sat and waited. When Emma's stomach rumbled a little before noon, she reached for the bag of donuts and ate a few munchkins. She knew they could be sitting there all day, if Sean didn't go anywhere at lunchtime.

But a half-hour later, the front door opened, and Sean stepped out and they watched him walk to his car. The Lamborghini was parked right by the front door. He started the engine, backed up, and then drove out of the lot. A moment later, Emma did the same.

"Now, slow down a little and stay back. You don't want him to notice you're following him."

"Okay." Emma stepped on the brake and slowed until Sean was way ahead, but still visible. They followed him onto Resnik Road and then Commerce Way and then turned onto the highway, Route 3, heading toward Boston.

Plymouth was so big that it took up five exits along Route 3. They drove along at a good distance for two exits before following Sean off the highway and immediately into the parking lot of Carmella's restaurant.

"Oh, good, I love Carmella's." Mickey seemed pleased with Sean's choice.

Emma parked at the other end of the lot, so they had a good view of the front door. They watched as Sean parked and walked into the restaurant.

"So, now we just wait for him to come out and see if he walks out with anyone?" Emma asked.

Mickey was already unbuckling his seatbelt. "Nope. Now we go eat lunch. Come on."

"Oh!" Emma grabbed her purse and followed Mickey inside.

When they reached the hostess stand, Mickey looked around the restaurant. The main dining room was on the left and the bar area on the right, with tables as well. Sean was in the bar area and had just been seated at a table by the window. It looked like he was waiting for someone as the waitress filled the water glass across from him.

"Would you like the main room or the bar area?" the hostess, a smiling, older woman asked.

"The bar area please, by a window, if possible," Mickey said.

"Right this way." She led them to a table next to a window and three tables away from where Sean sat. She handed them menus and as she walked away, Mickey lowered his voice.

"We'll want to order quickly and pay early. So, if he's on the move before we finish, we can duck out easily."

"No problem. I'm starving anyway." When their waitress came to the table, she set down a basket of hot, Italian-seasoned focaccia bread and a bowl of dipping oil, with red pepper flakes and a mound of parmesan cheese in the middle. Mickey immediately snapped off a chunk of bread and dipped it in the oil. Emma did the same. And they put their orders in right away. A chicken parmesan sub for Mickey and a stuffed pepper and salad for Emma.

As their waitress went off to the kitchen, they both noticed a woman walk in and with a big smile, head straight to Sean's table. She looked to be a little older than Emma, maybe mid-thirties with long, bleached blond hair, tight-fitting jeans and a low-cut sweater that showed off her ample assets.

"Can you get a picture?" Mickey asked.

Emma nodded and held her cell phone up as if she was checking messages, and aimed it carefully at Sean and the woman. She snapped several pictures and jumped a little in her chair as she captured the money shot—Sean pulled the woman in for a hug and a kiss hello, on the lips.

Mickey sensed her excitement.

"Let me see."

She handed him the phone, and he thumbed through the pictures and smiled when he saw the final shot.

"Good job, Emma. Looks like Sydney's suspicions were right on."

"So, are we done then? Is that all we need?"

"Not yet. We'll finish out the day. See where he goes after work. Maybe we can get a few more shots. My back is to them, so you'll have to keep an eye on their body language during lunch. Are they flirty? Could be they are just friends and haven't seen each other in a while."

Emma raised her eyebrows. "Friends that kiss on the lips? Doubtful."

Mickey shrugged. "I've seen it all. You never do know."

Their lunch came soon after and they both dug in. Emma had been to Carmella's once before, but had been to their sister restaurants, Mamma Mia's, many times, and her favorite thing was the stuffed peppers. It was the same recipe in both places—ground beef mixed with breadcrumbs, raisins, pine nuts and parmesan cheese, smothered in red sauce and more cheese.

Mickey seemed happy with his lunch too. Emma

noticed as they ate that Sean and his lunch companion seemed to be having a very good time. He kept reaching for her hand and squeezing it, and she was smiling and laughing the entire time. It looked like a date to Emma and not a first date. It seemed like they knew each other very well.

Emma filled Mickey in as they ate. "He's holding her hand again. I'm surprised he met her in public like this."

"Most people don't go out to lunch in the middle of the day, or if they do, they stay close to their office. This is typical behavior for an affair. He went to the next town over, where he's unlikely to run into anyone this time of day."

"Oh, I guess that makes sense."

"Lunch is more common than dinner, when you don't want to be seen," Mickey said.

They finished up as Sean's food was delivered, so they ordered a dessert to split while they waited. Or rather, Mickey ordered dessert and insisted that Emma have a bite. She sipped a black coffee as he ate his cannoli.

"You're awfully tiny there, Emma. Stick with me and I'll fatten you up. Have a bite. You really have to try this."

She tried a bite and agreed that it was delicious. But she knew she needed to be careful. It would be very easy to gain weight as everyone she knew in Plymouth seemed to be obsessed with food.

Mickey tried to pay the bill when the waitress brought it, but Emma was faster. "This is on the house. Or rather, it's on Sydney—expenses that she'll be charged."

He chuckled at that. "All right, then."

They waited until Sean and his date left and then immediately followed them outside. Emma had her phone ready to snap a few shots. They walked slowly to their car and Emma managed to get several good shots of Sean with his date. There was no doubt, by the way he had his arms around her and the very long goodbye kiss that they shared, that they were more than friends.

They climbed back into Emma's car and followed Sean back to his office. Emma stayed far back and even went around the block so he wouldn't see them pull into the lot. Once he was inside, they found a new spot, further away in the lot, but still with an eye on the door.

Once they were settled, Emma pulled out her phone, and they went through the pictures. She was excited by the shots and glad that they had managed to find some solid evidence for their client. She emailed the photos to her mother, and she called Emma back a moment later.

"Good job, honey. I spoke briefly with that Belinda Russell. She's going to stop into the office tomorrow morning to meet with us. I'm not sure about this case though."

"Why not?"

"Well, it's not typical. But, it sounds like your father was getting quite the reputation for more difficult investigations. I'm just not sure if this is something we want to take on. Remember the woman that Matt mentioned the other night? The one that went missing?"

"The lawyer?"

"Yes. It's her mother. She thinks the police have given up, and she wants answers."

"Oh."

"Right. That was my first response, too. I told her we'd meet with her though and then decide if we think we can help."

"Okay. We'll talk more in the morning then."

Emma ended the call and glanced at Mickey, who was clearly waiting for her to fill him in. So she did. He listened and then nodded.

"That's what I was referring to earlier. Your father was very effective, and more of these types of cases have been coming his way. But he sometimes worked a little too close to the edge."

"So, you don't think we should take on this case, then?"

Mickey grinned. "I didn't say that. We just need to be careful."

———

EMMA AND MICKEY TOOK TURNS READING ON THEIR phones for the rest of the afternoon and chatting now and then. One person always kept a close eye on the front door. Emma didn't expect that they'd see Sean before five, but at a few minutes past four, he surprised her by walking outside and hopping into his car.

Mickey was chuckling at something he was reading on his phone when she got his attention by starting the engine.

"Looks like we're on the move," she said.

"Hmm. Interesting. His wife said he's never home before six or seven."

They followed Sean back onto the highway, but this time he headed the opposite way, further south into Plymouth. He exited onto Long Pond Road and they followed as he turned onto Home Depot Drive.

"Maybe he's going shopping at Home Depot?" Emma said.

"I doubt it."

Mickey was right. Sean turned as though he was heading to Home Depot and at the last minute took a left into the parking lot for the Hilton Garden Inn.

"He's going to a hotel? After having a lunch date?" Emma was surprised.

They parked and watched Sean walk into the lobby.

"What now?" Emma asked.

"Now we wait for him to come out. And we pay attention to who else goes in."

Five minutes later, a white Mini Cooper pulled into the lot. They watched as a pretty brunette woman in her mid-thirties got out of the car. She was fashionably dressed in a black suit with a pink silk shirt and kitten heels.

Emma didn't pay that close attention once she realized it wasn't the blond woman from the restaurant. She did like her outfit though and had always admired Mini-Cooper cars.

"His date is probably already in the hotel, right?" Emma asked.

"It's possible. Or maybe that woman was his date,"

Mickey said.

"You really think so? I assumed he'd be meeting the blond woman from earlier."

"One thing about this job. You can never assume. People surprise me all the time. It's true what they say— truth is really stranger than fiction."

An hour and a half later, with no signs of Sean, Emma found herself reaching for the bag of donuts again.

"Pass those over here, if you please," Mickey said.

They were both munching on donuts when the front door opened and the brunette woman they'd seen earlier walked out, and a few steps behind her, was Sean. They stopped briefly at her car and he gave her a quick hug, no lingering kiss this time. But still, Emma was shocked. She managed to get quite a few shots with her phone, though. And when Sean drove off, they followed him from a distance and watched as he pulled into his own driveway at a few minutes past six. As if he was just getting home from work.

"What a jerk!" Emma said as she turned the car to head back to the office.

"Yep. We have everything we need though."

When they reached the office parking lot, Emma dropped Mickey off by his cute convertible.

"See you tomorrow, Mickey. Oh, the new prospective client, Belinda, is coming in at nine, if you'd like to be there for the meeting."

"I wouldn't miss it. See you in the morning, and good job, Emma. Your father would have been proud."

CHAPTER 4

By the time Emma got home after her first day at the agency, she was exhausted. Who knew that sitting around in a car all day could be so tiring? She heated up a can of soup, watched TV for a bit, and went to bed early.

She woke the next day at her normal time of just about six. Since she wasn't due to be in the office for a few hours and the sun was shining, she decided to make herself a big cup of coffee and head out to the beach for a walk.

Even at that early hour, there were already a few others out walking. Emma sipped her coffee as she walked along the water's edge, enjoying the sound of the waves and the feel of the soft morning breeze across her face. She walked the length of the beach, stopping when she reached the river that ran into the ocean. She made her way back to her cottage and had a second cup of coffee on the deck and wondered what the day might bring.

She'd looked up Belinda Russell and her daughter's case online and was intrigued. Part of her hoped they'd have a chance to investigate, but the other half agreed with her mother that this type of case might be a bit over their heads. Although, they did have Mickey. Emma knew that he'd been an excellent detective for many years and probably worked on his share of missing person cases, even murders. But did he want to deal with something like that now?

Emma pulled into the office parking lot at eight thirty and was surprised to see Mickey's car was already there. When she walked in the office, he waved hello as he pulled a sugar-dusted lemon cruller from a paper bag. Emma smiled as she saw the telltale trail of powdered sugar already on his desk. Mickey had already had at least one donut. She said hello as she settled at the main desk by the window.

"You're in early," she commented as she turned on the computer.

"I'm interested to hear what this Belinda woman has to say. Looked her up online when I got home last night. It's a damn shame. Her only daughter."

"I know. And the police really haven't turned up much of anything yet. Not that they've shared, anyway."

"It's not usually good news when someone goes missing for this long." Mickey looked up as the front door opened and Emma's mother walked in. Emma stood to give her mother her usual spot, but she waved her off. "Go ahead and stay there. I'm going to make a pot of coffee. You can check the email for us."

Emma sat back down and scrolled through the email that had come in overnight. It was mostly junk mail and a message from John Simon at Workman's Insurance asking her mother to give him a call.

"Who's John Simon?" Emma asked when her mother returned a few minutes later with a cup of coffee. She settled on a long, brown leather sofa in the middle of the room. There were matching armchairs on either side, and that's where they usually met with clients.

"He's one of our best clients. Your father said that he had work from him pretty steadily. Mostly workman's comp investigations. People that say they are too injured to work."

Mickey laughed. "Wait until you go on one of those. Some of these guys that say their backs are so bad they can barely move—we catch them lifting all kinds of heavy stuff."

Her mother smiled. "That's the kind of case that I'm more comfortable with us handling. I'm not so sure about Belinda Russell's. If the police can't find out what happened to her daughter, I'm not sure we'd be able to do any better."

Emma nodded. "I was thinking the same thing."

Mickey looked at both of them and wasn't laughing anymore. "Don't rule it out until after we talk to her. Your father and I cracked quite a few cases together." He sat up tall in his chair. "I have done this once or twice, you know. I know my way around a real police investigation."

"Well, yes, of course you do," her mother said quickly. "I didn't mean to imply that you didn't. But both Emma and I are new at this and well, neither one of us knows the first thing about an actual murder investigation if that's what this turns out to be. A missing person case is very different." She bit her lower lip and Emma knew she was worried that she'd offended Mickey and also worried in general about taking on a case that they couldn't handle.

But Mickey reminding them about his police background made Emma curious to see what they could do. It might be much more interesting than sitting in a parking lot waiting to catch a cheating spouse.

"Let's wait and see what Belinda Russell has to say, Mom, before we decide anything."

Her mother nodded. "Fair enough."

They all looked up a moment later when the front door opened and an attractive woman with white blond hair stepped into the office. She looked to be in her mid-sixties, which seemed about right as the missing woman was thirty-nine.

"Mrs. Russell?" Emma asked.

The older woman smiled. "Yes, I'm Belinda."

Emma's mother stood and welcomed her. "It's so nice to meet you. I'm Cindy, this is my daughter, Emma, and this is Mickey. He's a former detective and has worked with my husband for many years. Please have a seat. Would you like some coffee? I'm going to add a splash to my cup."

"It's very nice to meet you all too. Yes, thank you. I think I will have a cup, just black please, no sugar." Belinda sat in one of the armchairs. Mickey sat in the other and Emma moved over to the sofa. A moment later, her mother joined them, set Belinda's coffee mug on the table and sat beside Emma.

"Thank you for agreeing to meet with me," Belinda said. "I'm very sorry about your loss. Fred was good friends with my husband, Joe. He passed just last year as well. So, that's why I thought to reach out. Joe always said Fred and Mickey could find anyone. He was impressed with Fred's stories."

Emma smiled. Her father had always loved to talk about his work. He was proud of what he did and he'd been good at it.

"Emma and I are still learning the ropes, we're nowhere near Fred's level of skill, but we do have Mickey's experience and expertise to help guide us."

"I know it's not going to be the same, but I thought that maybe you could try. Like you said, you do have Mickey's help." Belinda glanced his way and he nodded.

"What can you share with us about what's been done so far and where things sit with the investigation?" Mickey asked.

Belinda took a deep breath. "First of all, I know it doesn't look good. It's been too long now and what they have found, well, I just don't know what to think."

"Take your time and start at the beginning," Mickey encouraged her.

"My daughter, Nancy, recently turned thirty-nine, and she was doing so well. She made partner earlier this year, and they loved her at her company. Everyone loved her. Nancy was always such a hard-worker and her best friend, Sheila, worked at the law firm too. She was the office manager. Nancy and Sheila had gone out for drinks and dinner after work, the night she went missing."

"When did they discover she was missing?" Mickey asked.

"She didn't go into work the next day. And when Sheila called Nancy's cell phone and home phone, she didn't answer and she didn't call back. It wasn't like Nancy at all. She was usually the first person in the office. Sheila called the police and when they went to the house, they saw that the garage door was unlocked and Nancy's car was missing." She paused for a moment and then her eyes grew damp and it was hard for her to speak again. Finally, she said, "They found pepper spray residue on the inside of the garage door. The police said they suspected that someone was waiting for her in the garage and surprised her when she got out of her car. She wasn't dating anyone that I was aware of. She lived alone, and she always carried pepper spray with her."

"I'm so sorry, Belinda," Emma's mother said. "Did they find the car?"

Belinda nodded. "Yes, they found it two days later, in the parking lot of an apartment complex a few streets over. They found one of Nancy's earrings in the trunk. At first, they thought it was a robbery, but after a week, they admitted it was probably something else, possibly worse." She looked around the room at the three of them and her voice broke. "I know she's probably gone. I just want answers, to know what happened and to get justice for Nancy."

"What kind of updates are the police giving you?" Mickey asked.

"I think they were very good, at first. They searched everywhere and talked to everyone at Nancy's company. But everyone loved Nancy. They didn't turn up anything at all. I'm not sure how hard they are still looking, at this point."

"The longer someone is missing, the harder it is to find them," Mickey said.

"Yes, they said that. It's just so discouraging. I was hoping that maybe you all could help. Or at least try to help?"

Emma wanted to help, but worried that they wouldn't be able to do anything more than the police had already done.

"Belinda, I'd really like to help. I just worry that we won't be able to do better than what the police have already done," Emma's mother said.

"We could try, but she's right, there are no guarantees," Mickey added.

"I understand that. But, if you're willing, I'd still like you to try. I can write you a check for a retainer for the first month. I'd like this to be a priority and I can pay you well. It's worth it to me. I hope this will be sufficient." She wrote out a check and handed it Emma's mother, whose eyes widened at the amount.

"We'd be happy to try to help you, Belinda. Thank you for trusting us. We'll get started on this today."

Belinda stood and shook everyone's hands as she said goodbye.

"Thank you. I'll keep you posted if I hear anything further from the police as well."

Once the door shut behind her, Emma got a look at the check and her jaw dropped. She showed it to Mickey, and he whistled softly. "She's not fooling around."

"So, where do we start with this, Mickey?" Emma asked.

"Pull up a chair and we'll make our game plan."

FOR THE NEXT FEW HOURS, MICKEY WALKED HER through the databases they used for skip-tracing cases. Emma had known that her father had access to various databases they could search to find information on people, but when she was younger, she was never allowed to actually run the searches as they were meant for licensed investigators only. She needed to actually work as an investigator for three years before she could get licensed. In the meantime, she would work under Mickey and his license was good for the whole office.

He walked her through how to use the three databases he and her father had liked to use most, Tracers, TLO, and IRB.

"Tracers is my favorite. But I like to use them all, so we don't miss anything. It's best for when someone goes on the run though, when they move leaving a pile of debt behind them and don't want to be found. There's always a trail. Eventually they surface with a new mailing address or phone number."

"So, this probably isn't going to help us find Nancy?" Emma said.

"Probably not. From all accounts, it doesn't sound like she willingly went anywhere. But it will rule out her taking off. Sometimes people do just up and leave and start over somewhere else."

Emma heard the whirring sound of the printer and a moment later her mother walked over and handed them a sheet of paper with names and phone numbers printed on it. "Belinda just emailed this over. It's a list of everyone in Nancy's life. Friends, co-workers, ex-boyfriends. She said the police have talked to all of them and didn't turn up anything." Before she walked back to her desk she added, "Oh, and the girls are coming over for drinks tonight, why don't you join us, honey? They'd love to see you."

"Sure, that sounds fun." Emma turned her attention to Mickey. "So, what do we do with this?"

He grinned. "We start dialing and asking for meetings."

"Will they talk to us if they've already talked to the police?"

"Some will. Some won't. They don't have to like they do with the police."

Mickey divided up the list, which wasn't all that long. He called Nancy's boss, Justin Powell, and her co-worker and her best friend, Sheila, the office manager. He also had her neighbors on either side, the Richardsons and the Cunninghams.

Emma had Nancy's two ex-boy friends, Ed and Tony.

She listened to Mickey make his calls first. He had to leave messages for everyone at the law firm. No one took his call, but he got through to both of the neighbors and they both agreed to meet with him that afternoon.

Emma had to leave a message for Ed but Tony agreed to meet with them the following day.

After lunch, Mickey and Emma headed out to meet with Nancy's neighbors.

"Do you think they might know something? Was she close to her neighbors?" Emma wondered out loud as she drove to the first house.

"Even if they didn't know her well, they might have noticed if something was off with her normal routine, people coming and going. If someone was there in the garage when she got home, maybe someone noticed a strange car hanging around the neighborhood."

But after spending close to an hour with the Richardsons and then the Cunninghams, they learned nothing that they didn't already know. Both couples were older and didn't know Nancy all that well.

"She's a lovely girl, but we almost never saw her. She works such long hours at that job of hers. Or she used to," Joyce Richardson said. "Do you think something awful has happened to her? That poor girl." She squeezed her husband's hand tight and looked close to tears.

"We don't know much of anything yet. That's why her mother hired us. She's anxious to find her daughter, to find answers to what happened," Mickey said.

Joyce nodded. "I wish I could be more helpful. I hope you find her."

Their visit with the Cunninghams went similarly. They also thought Nancy was a lovely girl, but rarely saw her. And didn't notice anything that evening.

When they left, Emma was discouraged, but Mickey wasn't. "I didn't think we'd learn much from them. But, you never know. It's the people that were really close to her that might have some answers. Or can at least point us in the right direction."

Emma turned on the radio as they drove back to the office. She hoped that they'd have better luck the next day when they met with Nancy's ex-boyfriends. Mickey was on the phone telling his wife, Betty, that he'd be happy to pick up some milk for her at the store and that he was looking forward to her chicken pot pies for supper, when the news came on the radio.

"This is breaking news. The body of missing Plymouth woman, Nancy Eldridge has been found, washed up on the shore where Eel River meets Plymouth Harbor. No further information is available at this time."

CHAPTER 5

Cindy stopped by Wood's Seafood when she left the office and picked up a pound of cooked cocktail shrimp and homemade cocktail sauce. She also picked up some cheese and crackers at The Market when she reached the Pinehills. The Market was the neighborhood store that had a bit of everything, including a very nice cheese section. She grabbed a few bottles of wine at the connected liquor store as well.

The girls were coming at six-thirty and it didn't take long for her to get ready for them. She opened a bottle of red wine, dumped the shrimp on a platter and the cocktail sauce in a small dish. And she made a cheese tray with the various cheeses and crackers. At six twenty-eight, she poured herself a glass of cabernet and took a sip.

Everyone arrived within a few minutes of each other. Lee brought chips and salsa, and Rachel brought a big bowl of homemade guacamole. Emma came rushing in with a bottle of chardonnay and a container of Marcona almonds tossed in olive oil and salt from The Market.

They gathered in the kitchen around the island and set all the food in the center. Cindy poured wine for everyone except Lee, who brought her favorite vodka and soda. Lee and Rachel fussed over Emma, giving her hugs and catching up before they all settled onto chairs around the island and dove into the snacks.

"Did you hear they found that missing girl?" Lee said as she dipped a chip into the guacamole.

"I heard that on the news earlier, so sad," Rachel said.

"We actually just started working on her case today," Cindy said. "Her mother met with us at the office. She was frustrated that the police hadn't found her yet."

"What does that mean for your case now?" Lee asked. "Will she still want you to investigate? I mean, the police will be all over it now, I would think?"

"I'll call her first thing in the morning, to offer our condolences and of course tell her we'd be happy to let the police take over."

"Mom was hesitant to take her case, as it was," Emma added.

"I was. I had a bad feeling that it might end up like this, and I'm not sure we should be involved. The police can handle it."

"We do a lot of work with the law firm she worked at," Rachel said. "They actually just called us right before I was about to walk out the door. They need another temp to start this Friday. Someone went out on maternity leave earlier than expected."

"What kind of work?" Emma asked.

"Secretarial, typing, filing, answering phones. Do you know anyone?"

Emma laughed. "No. I don't know a soul anymore around here."

Cindy smiled. "If she didn't already have a job, Emma could do that with her eyes closed. You worked in a few law firms in L.A., didn't you, honey?"

"I did. I did a lot of temping when I was in between acting work, which was most of the time. My typing speed is pretty good!"

"Well, if you ever want to temp, let me know. We can put you to work right away." Rachel laughed. "How are you liking it at the agency?"

Emma's face lit up. "I'm really liking it. I always liked helping my dad out when I was younger, but it's more fun to actually do the job." She told them about the surveillance job she'd done with Mickey and the cheating husband they'd followed.

"Wow, two different women in one day. That's crazy," Lee said.

"How did the wife take it?" Rachel asked.

Cindy sighed. "That's one part of the job I don't care for. Even though she suspected what was going on, she still broke down and cried when I talked with her on the phone and told her what we'd learned. I'm sure she was hoping we wouldn't find anything."

"What is she going to do about it?" Lee asked.

"I think she's going to file for divorce. She said it's just too much to forgive. She could never trust him again."

"No. How could you?" Rachel agreed.

"I can't imagine," Emma said.

They chatted and laughed for another two hours. The time flew by. Emma told stories of her time in L.A. and had them all laughing. Cindy sighed with happiness. It was really a perfect night with her girlfriends and her daughter. She was so happy that Emma was back in Plymouth, and she hoped it would work out and that she'd stay.

EMMA LEFT HER MOTHER'S HOUSE A LITTLE AFTER NINE. She was full and yawning as she pulled onto Taylor Avenue. Parking was at a premium with the houses like Emma's on the sand, as there was no normal driveway. But she did have access to a parking spot, right off Taylor Avenue and just a short walk to her cottage.

This time of year, many of the cottages were empty as they were only used during the summer months and not winterized. Emma had never felt unsafe in the area, but it was a bit deserted and so when she saw a dark figure walking near her cottage, she stopped short for a moment.

But when the person took another step, and she saw his face in the moonlight, she recognized him. She also realized he was heading to the cottage next to hers.

"Brady? Is that you?"

He stopped short, turned around and broke into a grin when he saw her.

"Emma? What are you doing here? You back in town visiting the family?"

"Back in town to stay for a while. I just moved into this cottage a few days ago."

He looked surprised. "Helen's place?"

She nodded. "She said she got tired of weekly rentals."

"I heard about your dad. I'm so sorry."

"Thanks. He and Helen were friends. So, that's how I ended up here. What about you? Are you living down here too?"

He nodded. "Yeah. I bought this cottage a few years ago. Got a good deal on it right after a big storm washed the deck away. Been here ever since. We'll have to catch up soon over few beers. I'd invite you over tonight, but you look like you're just coming home."

Emma smiled. "I'd love to catch up another time, definitely. I was just at my mom's and I'm about ready to fall into bed."

"Well, sleep tight, Emma. If you ever need anything, just give me a holler."

"I'll do that. Goodnight, Brady."

Emma let herself in and locked the door behind her. She was pleasantly surprised to discover that her neighbor was Brady Smith. They'd graduated high school together and ran in the same circle of friends. She'd always liked Brady. He was a nice guy, and she'd always found him attractive too with his green eyes and wavy dark blond hair. They'd never been single at the same time, so dating had never really crossed her mind, though. She was sure he was probably dating someone now, anyway. Brady had never been single for long.

She was glad to have a neighbor nearby that she knew. It would be fun to catch up with him, though it wouldn't be over a beer as he'd suggested. Her beer drinking days ended when she discovered wine in college. She smiled as she drifted off to sleep, picturing the two of them relaxing on her deck, watching the sunset and filling each other in on what they'd been up to since they'd last seen each other, at least five years ago.

CHAPTER 6

"I might as well have one of those donuts you brought," Mickey said. It was the next day, a little after eleven and Emma and Mickey were sitting in a different neighborhood, parked on the side of the road, waiting for their subject to leave his house and go somewhere. Emma handed Mickey the paper bag of donuts.

Mickey fished out a jelly donut and handed it back to her. "You're not going to join me? There's a lemon one in there and a chocolate one, too. Both excellent choices."

Emma sighed. She'd gone for a walk that morning and had a yogurt with her coffee. She thought she'd be able to resist. She'd brought them just because she knew Mickey loved them. Though lemon-filled was her favorite, so who was she kidding? She reached for it and Mickey grinned.

They'd been sitting there for over an hour and it was getting boring. The donuts helped.

"What if this guy never leaves his house today? Could be a long day," Emma said after she took a big bite. The donut was delicious.

"He'll probably go somewhere. They almost always do. Who wants to stay home all day?"

Their subject was Mark Thomas, aged thirty-two. He was a union sheet-metal worker and had been on a big construction site, a new office building in South Boston. He'd been injured on the job and had been out on workman's comp insurance for over six months. Supposedly his back was too injured to return to work. He claimed that he couldn't lift anything and could barely move. Most people recovered more quickly from an injury like his, so the insurance company wanted to confirm that he was as injured as he claimed.

"Is it common that people lie about this?" Emma asked.

Mickey chuckled. "More common than you might think. About half of these cases show that the person isn't as injured as they claim. We'll see about Mr. Thomas."

Emma was glad for Mickey's company. It would have been more boring if she'd been by herself. He kept her entertained with stories of his detective days. And at a few minutes past one, still with no sign of movement from the house, Mickey opened an insulated tote bag and pulled out two tuna fish sandwiches and a bag of potato chips. He handed one of the sandwiches to Emma. "Betty packed these for us."

"Oh, how nice of her." Emma hadn't planned beyond the donuts, but it was so thoughtful of Mickey's wife.

They munched their sandwiches in comfortable silence. Just as they were finishing up, Emma caught a glimpse of movement at the house. The front door opened and a tall, heavyset man with thinning brown hair and a Red Sox sweatshirt and jeans walked toward a truck in the driveway. He moved quickly, easily and got into the truck and started the engine.

"That's our guy. He's on the move."

Emma watched as his navy truck backed out of the driveway and headed down the street. He passed Emma's car and didn't even glance their way. Emma waited until he was down the road a way before pulling out and following him. She took care to keep at a safe distance.

They were in West Plymouth, in the newish Redbrook community. They drove out of Redbrook and followed the blue truck as it turned left on Long Pond Road. They drove along past Waverly Oaks and Crosswinds golf courses until they reached the Home Depot plaza.

Emma laughed as they turned into the parking lot. "Do you think he's going to the hotel too?" It was the same place they'd been to a few days prior.

Mickey laughed too. "Wouldn't that be something? I don't think so, though."

The truck did not turn left to go to the hotel, but kept going into the Home Depot parking lot and parked close to one of the entrances. They parked nearby, where they would have a good view of Mark returning to his vehicle. They watched him go into the store and waited. Twenty minutes later, he wheeled a cart to his truck that was loaded with gardening stuff. Huge bags of potting soil, a gardening shovel, and several bushes of some kind.

"How much do you think those big bags weigh?" Emma asked.

"At least forty pounds or so. A lot more than he says he can lift."

They watched as he easily lifted everything from the cart and put it in the back of his truck. Emma caught it all on video from her cell phone. He got in the truck and Emma glanced at Mickey.

"Do we keep following him, or is this enough?"

"It's probably enough, but let's see what he does next."

Emma followed the truck back to Redbrook and slowed way down so that he was way ahead. She assumed he was probably going home and didn't want him to notice the same car still behind him. When he reached his house, she drove past it, circled around and came back behind and down a few houses but where they still had a view of the house.

"Well, will you look at that. He's bringing everything outside by the front door. This should be interesting," Mickey said.

"Hmm. I don't think he's supposed to be doing that," Emma said.

Mark slammed a shovel into the ground, pulling up grass and dirt. He cleared a whole area. Then opened one of the bags of soil and dumped it on the ground. They watched as he planted all the bushes, bending and lifting, over and over. And then, he went into the garage and carried out several big rocks that he placed around the bushes.

Mickey shook his head. "Nothing wrong with that boy's back."

"So, what happens now?" Emma asked.

"We'll turn in all of our video from today to the insurance company, and they will have a little chat with Mr. Thomas. I suspect he'll be back on the job very soon—and he may have a sizable bill, to repay some of the monies he collected. I think we can head back to the office now. Looks like he's done with his gardening project."

———————

CINDY TURNED WHEN SHE HEARD THE OFFICE DOOR OPEN and saw Emma and Mickey walk in.

"How did it go?"

"It was almost too easy," Mickey said. "He made the mistake of going to Home Depot and then gardening. We got loads of video." He and Emma both looked pleased.

Cindy smiled. "That's great. I'll email to let them know."

"I'll upload the video now." Emma sat and opened her laptop.

"Well, I'm going to be on my way. Any word from Nancy's mother? Are we focusing on that again tomorrow?" Mickey asked.

"I spoke with Belinda briefly, about an hour ago. She's having a hard time with this, as you can imagine. We both thought it was a good idea to put things on hold for at least a week or two. To let the police start their investigation. Now that it's a murder, it will get a higher priority. She still may want our help, if the police don't get anywhere."

Mickey nodded. "I saw in the paper this morning that her funeral is on Monday. Were you both planning to go to the wake? Might be a good idea for all of us to be there and to pay attention. Never know what we might notice."

"I hadn't even thought about going," Emma said.

"Yes, I'm planning to go. Emma, you can ride with me or just meet us there. It's at Cartmell's, across from Christ Church. The wake is Sunday afternoon and the funeral service Monday morning. I don't think we should go to the funeral, that's usually just immediate family and close friends."

"Just the wake is good," Mickey confirmed.

"Oh, Belinda mentioned that Nancy's boss, Justin Powell, insisted on paying for the funeral. Isn't that nice? She said the whole office feels horrible and since Nancy worked such long hours there, he felt it was the least he could do."

"He's a generous guy from what I hear. Big spender, too. Buddy of mine keeps a small SeaRay at the marina, has had it there for years. We go fishing now and then. Anyway, he said Powell got a new, huge yacht this year. And he has more than one flashy sports car. I don't know what they are but they're both red and look expensive."

"Belinda thinks pretty highly of him. He adored Nancy and paid her very well, she said."

"Did she say if they have any suspects?" Mickey asked.

Cindy shook her head. "No. She said they don't have any yet."

CHAPTER 7

E mma met Matt and Dana for after-work drinks and dinner Friday night at Su Casa on Main Street. It was a few doors down from Sam Diego's, the Tex-Mex restaurant that Emma had been going to forever. But Matt and Dana said she had to try this new place.

They sat outside in a very pretty covered area with twinkling lights. They all ordered margaritas, street corn, and a tuna appetizer to share. The street corn was grilled and slathered with a creamy cheese and spices and was insanely delicious. They all got different small tacos as well.

"Order whatever you like, but you have to get at least one fried avocado taco," Matt said.

She did, and he was right. Once they were done eating, they ordered another round of Margaritas and Emma felt so relaxed, full, and happy.

"I'm really glad to be back," she admitted.

Matt laughed. "Well, it's about time. We all missed you. I hoped you'd come home sooner, but I know you had to give it your best shot. How are you feeling about that. Any regrets?"

"No. Not really. Would I have liked it to work out? Yes, absolutely. But so many people want to be actors. Very few actually make it. And to be honest, I didn't love the lifestyle out there. I missed New England, missed you guys."

"I know Mom is glad you're back," Matt said.

"Is it fun working together?" Dana asked.

Emma thought about it for a moment and grinned. "It is. It's nice. We work together, but not really together. She talks to clients and manages the office, and Mickey and I are out in the field. Mickey's great." She filled them in on the surveillance work they'd done so far.

"That sounds interesting," Dana said. She glanced at Matt. "You never wanted to be a part of that?"

Matt shook his head. "No, that was always Dad's thing, and Emma's. I always had the cars. It's all good."

"Any updates on that Nancy woman? I know it's a murder case now. It's been all over the news," Dana said.

"No, not really. We're kind of on hold with it now that the police are making it a priority. She may want us to start up again if they don't get anywhere after a few weeks."

"Do you really think you guys could help if the police can't figure it out?" Matt asked. He looked doubtful, and Emma didn't blame him.

"I honestly don't know. Mom and I think it might be over our heads, but Mickey seems pretty keen on it and he's the one with the experience, so it might be fun to at least try."

"Are you sure it's safe, though? Investigating a murder seems potentially a little more dangerous than the usual types of things you do," Dana said.

Emma smiled. "I'm sure. We're very careful."

"Yeah, Mickey knows what he's doing," Matt said. "How's the cottage? Are you all settled in?"

"Yes! I love it. I need to have you guys over soon. Maybe next weekend. If it's nice out, we can have a cookout on Saturday or Sunday."

"That would be fun. I haven't been over to White Horse Beach in a while, and I'd love to see your place," Dana said.

"Matt, that reminds me. Do you know Brady Smith? He was in my grade. I ran into him when I was coming home the other night. He lives next door. Said he bought his cottage a few years ago."

Matt frowned. "Brady Smith? Yeah, I know him. I didn't realize he owned the place next to you. If I did, I might have suggested you rent somewhere else."

"Why? I haven't seen him in years, but I always liked him in high school. We had some of the same friends."

"Well, he's not that bad personally, but he's not someone I'd ever want my sister to date."

"I wasn't planning on dating him. But what did he do?"

Matt sighed. "He dated a good friend, Caroline, for a

few years. Everyone thought they were on their way to getting engaged, and then one day he broke things off and moved out of town. I didn't realize he was back."

"Oh. Do you know what happened?"

"No idea. He never really gave Caroline a good reason. Just said he was sorry, but he couldn't do it anymore and she knew why. But, she said, she had no idea why. She was pretty messed up about it for a while."

"So, he left and came back. What does he do for work?"

"Some kind of consultant, software, I think. So he travels a lot. Just steer clear of him. I don't need my baby sister getting her heart broken, okay?"

Emma laughed. "No need to worry about that. So, what else is new?"

EMMA SAID GOODBYE TO MATT AND DANA A LITTLE AFTER nine and headed home to White Horse Beach. The area was quiet and as she walked to her cottage, she glanced at Brady's place next door. It was totally dark. He was either traveling or out for the evening. Emma yawned as she unlocked her door and stepped inside. She was ready to fall into bed.

The next day, after sleeping in until eight, she took a walk on the beach with her coffee and decided to go join the gym she used to belong to years ago. Plymouth Fitness was the nicest one in the area, with a pool and racquetball courts, every kind of machine under the sun and lots of classes.

She signed up and put her purse and towels in a locker before heading to one of the elliptical machines. She did thirty minutes on that before going downstairs to work a little with the free weights. She was on her last set of squats when she heard a familiar voice and looked up to see her friend Tess chatting with an older woman by one of the weight machines.

She hadn't seen Tess in years. They'd been good friends in high school and through college, even though they went to different schools. They'd lost touch once Emma moved to L.A., but she'd wondered how Tess was doing and had been meaning to look her up. Tess looked her way and broke into a grin. She said goodbye to the woman she was talking to and walked over to Emma.

"Emma McCarthy! What are you doing here?"

"I moved home. I haven't been back long. How are you? Are you still working here?" Tess was a personal trainer and, of course, was in fantastic shape. She was about 5'5" and had big blue eyes, wavy blonde hair and a trim, toned figure. She was full of energy and always upbeat.

"It's so great to see you! Yes, I'm still working here. My business is going well. We need to catch up. I've been married and divorced!"

"Oh my gosh. We really do need to catch up. You married Tommy, right? Tommy Harrison?"

Tess nodded. "The one and only. I should have known better. But it's over and it's all good. I have a little girl.

Hayley is three, and she's a handful, but so cute. You have to meet her."

"I'd love to. Where are you living?"

"I'm in White Horse Beach, the condos on the hill." Emma knew the ones she meant. They were at the end of Taylor Avenue and were high on a hill, overlooking the beach.

"I'm right around the corner." She told her about the cottage and her neighbor. "Remember Brady Smith?"

"Of course I remember, Brady. He's a great guy. He has a membership here too. I think he's part of the early bird crowd. The guys that come in before work."

"My brother's not a fan." She told Tess what Matt had said about his friend Caroline.

"Hmm. Brady always seemed like a nice guy to me. You never really know what is going on with people's relationships, though. Maybe Matt didn't have the whole story."

"Probably not. So, let's definitely get together soon." They put each other's numbers in their phones and made a tentative plan to meet up the next morning for coffee at Emma's. Emma was glad that she'd run into Tess. She really didn't have any other friends in Plymouth, and she missed having girlfriends to do things with. She loved hanging out with her mother and her friends, but it wasn't the same.

WHEN EMMA WALKED INTO HER MOTHER'S KITCHEN LATER

that afternoon, Lee and Rachel were already there. Her mother was looking through her shoes in the front hall closet and finally found the ones she was looking for. They were all wearing black, and Emma asked if her mother's friends knew Nancy or her mother.

"My company does a lot of business with the law firm, Nancy worked at," Rachel said.

"Belinda goes to my church. I don't know her well, but I can't imagine what she's going through. I wanted to show my support," Lee said.

"Are we ready to go? I'll drive," Emma's mother offered.

It took them about fifteen minutes to get to the funeral home, and Emma wasn't surprised to see that there was already a long line of people waiting to pay their respects. They parked and joined the line. A few minutes later, Mickey and his wife, Betty, arrived and joined them in line. Mickey looked distinguished in his black suit with a lavender tie. His wife, Betty, had short curls the same white shade as Mickey. She wore an elegant black dress, and she came and chatted with them all as they waited.

Finally, they made their way inside and went through the receiving line where Belinda and several family members were standing. Belinda was smiling, but she looked numb and her eyes were red. They all told her how sorry they were and then went into the back of the room where people were talking softly and saying hello to people they hadn't seen in a while.

"See that guy over there, in the dark gray suit,

maroon tie? That's Justin Powell, Nancy's boss," Mickey said.

Emma followed his gaze. Justin stood out. He was very tall, 6' 3" or 6' 4" she guessed. He looked to be around fifty with a thick head of black hair that was wavy and graying slightly at the temples, but he had it slicked back with gel. His suit was clearly expensive, as was his watch and shoes. Justin dressed to be noticed. And he obviously liked nice things.

The woman by his side was dressed expensively too. She wore a conservative navy dress, but her very high heels were the infamous Christian Louboutins with their signature red soles. Her fire engine red purse was a Prada. And her diamond wedding ring was the biggest Emma had ever seen.

"Is that his…"

"Wife, yes. That's Deidre Powell. I suppose you could call them one of Plymouth's power couples, if Plymouth had such a thing," Mickey scoffed at the thought. Plymouth was not a stuffy town at all.

"Who's that?" Emma saw a woman who looked to be around forty who walked up to Justin and Deidre and had tears running down her face. Justin pulled her in for a hug while Deidre looked at the two of them coldly. After a moment, she walked outside. A man and woman walked over to the crying woman and Justin Powell and more hugs were exchanged. "Maybe they all work together?" she said.

Rachel overheard her and nodded. "That's Sheila, the office manager. She was best friends with Nancy. I think the other two are attorneys in the office. They're all broken up. Justin thought the world of her."

"His wife didn't look overly sad," Emma said.

"No, I don't imagine she would have. There are rumors that Justin has been unfaithful, and with all the time he spends in the office, I've heard he has had flings with some of his staff. If I've heard that, odds are Deidre has too. I don't know why she puts up with it."

"I can think of millions of reasons why," Mickey said.

"Right, money. But you'd think she'd do very well if they divorced," Rachel said.

"Unless there was a pre-nup?" Emma said.

"Good point," Rachel agreed. "He is a lawyer after all, and he has a reputation as a very good one. He's something of a celebrity lawyer—he has worked for some very famous people, in sports and politics."

"Did you ever fill that temp job you mentioned?" Emma asked. A sudden idea came to her.

"I filled one of them, but I still need one more person to go in for two days next week. It's just a short-term fill-in assignment for one of their secretaries."

Emma glanced at her mother. "We have a slow week next week, I think you said?"

Her mother nodded. "Yes, we have a few small things to work on, but we're not busy by any means."

"What if I did that temp job? It's just for a few days and maybe I can learn something by being there."

"You can go undercover, I love it!" Mickey said.

"I'm not sure that's a good idea," her mother said.

"If you could do that, I'll really owe you one. We have a shortage of good people right now," Rachel said.

"I'd love to do it." Emma was excited about the idea of going undercover.

"All right, I'll email you the address. Plan on being there Tuesday morning at eight-thirty sharp."

CHAPTER 8

Emma didn't have time for her morning beach walk on Tuesday because she spent twenty minutes trying to decide what to wear for her first day of the legal temporary assignment. She finally settled on a pair of navy pants, matching blazer, and a simple white jersey shirt.

She hadn't worn any of it since her last temp job a few months back. It was all from Banana Republic— simple, clean separates that managed to be somewhat casual but corporate enough for any office. Once that decision was made and she ran an iron over the pants and jacket, she made a mug of coffee and took it to the deck to get a few minutes of beach time.

The air was slightly cool and there was a heavy, misty fog that gave the whole beach a dreamy, semi-transparent look. Almost no one was walking the beach today other than a few diehard regulars and their dogs.

Emma's stomach felt a bit restless. Nerves, she

guessed, and made herself a quick peanut butter sandwich, which always seemed to help. She used to eat one before her auditions.

In a way, this was like an audition, as she was going to be playing a part and had to be convincing. She wasn't worried about being able to do the work, as she knew her office skills were pretty good. She was just slightly nervous about anyone making the connection to her father and Court Street Investigations. Though, as Mickey tried to assure her, no one really knew she was working there yet.

"Meow."

Emma turned at the sound and saw a skinny orange cat staring at her. He was sitting on the deck, facing her, and she looked at him in surprise. He meowed again, walked closer and rubbed his cheek against her leg.

"Well, hello there. Who are you? And where do you live?" She reached over and scratched the cat behind the ears, and he started to purr loudly. The cat had moved so quietly, as cats did, that she hadn't even noticed that he'd walked onto the deck. He wasn't wearing a collar, and he was very thin. But he was a big cat too, one of the biggest she'd seen. She guessed he was close to twenty pounds.

She broke off a piece of her sandwich and held it out to him. He sniffed and took a tentative bite, then twitched his tail and walked off. The sandwich was apparently not acceptable. The cat turned back for a final look before disappearing down the stairs. Emma wondered if he lived nearby and maybe just didn't have a collar. She'd never seen the cat before. She decided to pick up a box of dry food, in case he dropped by again.

She glanced at the time on her phone and realized she needed to get a move on if she was going to be at the law firm by eight-thirty.

She dressed quickly, then headed out and arrived at Foley, Watson, and Powell five minutes early. The law firm was located in a big, brick building in the Plymouth Industrial Park, just off Resnik Eoad. It wasn't far from the Colony Place shops and lots of fast-food places like Chipotle and Chick Fil A, so she had options if she wanted to zip out on her lunch break.

She'd done her research on the firm and knew that they were the largest in the area and had twenty lawyers covering the South Shore and Cape and Islands as well as Boston. She didn't know how many support staff, but guessed at least ten to fifteen, maybe more, depending on if attorneys shared or had their own assistants.

Rachel had told her to check in at the front desk and ask for Sheila, the office manager. She was the woman she'd seen crying at the funeral. Nancy's best friend.

Emma took a deep breath, then grabbed her Kate Spade navy and cream-colored purse and went inside. A young blond woman was just settling into her chair at the front desk and looked up in surprise when she saw Emma. Apparently they didn't get a lot of foot traffic first thing in the morning.

"Hello, can I help you with something?"

"Hi, I'm Emma McCarthy, from the temp agency. I was told to ask for Sheila?"

"Oh. Of course. Please have a seat. I'll let her know."

Emma settled into a leather padded chair, one of

about a dozen in the waiting area. She looked around the large lobby. It was elegantly appointed, with lots of dark leather, and a glass and chrome table with a stack of legal magazines and a copy of People. The walls were a soft ivory and there were a half dozen paintings, all seascapes of Plymouth Harbor. There were also a few photographs of Justin Powell with well-known figures like Tony Robbins, and New York Governor Andrew Cuomo.

She was just about to reach for the People magazine when Sheila walked into the lobby and smiled at her. "Emma McCarthy?"

Emma stood. "Yes, nice to meet you."

"Come on back with me and I'll show you what you'll be working on."

Emma followed her down a hallway to a small office adjacent to a much bigger one.

"That's my office there. If you have any questions, just come find me. You've transcribed dictation before?"

Emma nodded. "Yes, many times." Listening to tapes made by attorneys and typing it up was something she'd done at most of her temp assignments with law firms.

"Good. Have you used BigHand?"

Emma nodded. It was a common dictation service.

"Excellent. Here's the login information and you can use this headset." She handed a newish looking pair to Emma. "You'll see a bunch of recordings in the queue— all the lawyers here use it. We have a bit of a backlog now. So we'll have you focus on that for most of today and have you cover for Alyssa when she goes on lunch break at noon. Then you can take your break at one. Sound good?"

"Perfect."

"All right. If you have any issues, like I said, come find me." Sheila walked off and Emma put the headphones on and fired up the computer. She signed into BigHand, opened the first file and started typing. She typed all morning, until Sheila popped into her office at a quarter to twelve and suggested she sit with Alyssa for a few minutes, so she could show her what to do at the front desk.

"It's really not hard," Alyssa said, when Sheila walked off. "The phone system here is simple. You just answer when it rings and put the caller on hold for a moment while you check and see if the attorney is available for the call. If they are, click transfer and punch in their extension number. Here's the list."

It seemed straightforward enough. Emma just hoped she wouldn't accidentally disconnect instead of transferring. It had happened before.

"Why don't you take this call?" Alyssa suggested when the phone rang.

Emma answered and managed to transfer the call successfully.

"See, told you it was easy. Okay. I'm off then. See you in an hour." Alyssa scampered off, grabbing her coat and purse and heading out the front door.

Sheila came back a few minutes later with a thick manilla folder full of legal documents.

"These have all been scanned. In between calls, can

you run these through the shredder please? I'll have more for you to scan then shred tomorrow once you get through the dictation. I took a look at what you've done so far and you're going at a good clip. Nice job."

"Thank you." Sheila walked off as the phone rang and Emma hurried to answer it.

"Justin Powell in? Jake Gregory here." The voice was commanding. It sounded like he was used to people jumping when he spoke.

"I'll check for you, please hold a moment."

Emma punched Justin's line, and he picked up immediately, "Who's looking for me?"

"Jake Gregory is calling. Would you like me to put him through?"

"Yes! Of course." He sounded impatient, as if Emma should know Jake Gregory.

She quickly transferred the call and then answered two more in quick succession. A few people walked in after that, and she called back to let the attorneys know their clients were in the waiting room. It stayed steadily busy at the front desk. Emma didn't have a lot of time for shredding, but did what she could when the phones were quiet.

At twelve thirty, four attorneys walked out together, probably going to lunch, Emma assumed. One of them was Justin Powell. He did a double take when he saw Emma and came over to talk to her.

"I didn't realize it wasn't Alyssa calling me. You must be the temp Sheila brought in for a few days?"

Emma nodded. "Yes, I'm Emma McCarthy."

"So, you probably won't be at the front desk much, but just so you know, Jake Gregory is one of our best clients and I will always take his call, so just put him right through. The four of us are heading out to lunch at the 110 Grill around the corner." He introduced Emma to the other three attorneys, and she jotted down all their names so she could just take messages for them if anyone called while they were out.

Sheila walked up to the desk a moment later, with a sad look.

"I forgot to tell you this. It's unlikely as I think just about everyone knows by now, but in case anyone calls looking for Nancy Eldridge, please put them right through to me and I'll handle it."

"Of course. I'm so sorry. I read in the paper that she'd just recently made partner here," Emma said.

Sheila sighed. "It still doesn't seem real. She was a good friend of mine. My best friend, actually."

"Do the police have any idea what might have happened?" Emma asked.

The phone rang then and Emma held off answering for a moment, waiting for Sheila to speak.

"They don't seem to know much at all. They just keep asking all of us questions, but they don't seem to be getting anywhere, as far as I know. None of it makes any sense. Everyone loved Nancy."

Emma reached for the phone as Sheila walked away.

The hour went by quickly and at a few minutes before one, Alyssa returned.

"How did it go?" She asked as she settled into her chair and cracked open a can of Diet Coke.

"It was fine. Busy, so time went by fast."

Alyssa grinned. "It's better than way. The slow days are boring. But it's not slow around here often. I can take over now if you want to head out."

Emma stood. "Oh, by the way, Justin Powell and three other attorneys went to lunch. I would think they'll be back soon."

"Did they go to the 110?"

Emma nodded.

"I don't expect them back for at least another hour then. They like to take their time and have a drink or two, especially when they go there, as it's so close."

"I think if I had a drink at lunch, I'd want to take a nap after," Emma admitted.

Alyssa laughed. "You and me both."

Emma decided to get tacos from Chipotle and ordered on the app, then drove the short distance to pick it up. She thought about walking there, but since she had an hour for lunch, she had time to do a little shopping at Colony Place after she ate.

Her order was ready when she walked into Chipotle and as she left, she glanced next door at the 110 Grill. Justin Powell and the other attorneys were seated outside with a few other men. They were drinking martinis, talking loudly and laughing. There was no food on the table yet, so she guessed that Alyssa was right and they wouldn't be coming back any time soon.

She ate her lunch in the car, bought a new lip gloss

and blush at Sephora, went through the drive-thru at Starbucks and was back at the law firm a few minutes before two. The rest of the afternoon was uneventful, and she got most of the dictation done. There were just a few tapes left to finish in the morning. Sheila seemed pleased when she stopped by at five thirty to let her know they were done for the day.

"You did a great job. When you finish these up tomorrow, I'll have some scanning and file projects for the rest of the day. There might be some more work in a few weeks too, if you're interested. One of our assistants will be out on vacation."

CHAPTER 9

Thursday morning, Cindy stopped by The Market on her way into work and picked up some more coffee for the office and, while she was there, a box of freshly made raspberry crumb donuts caught her eye. She knew both Mickey and Emma would help her out with those.

Emma's car was already in the parking lot and Mickey pulled in right behind Cindy. They walked in together and Cindy set the box of donuts on the coffee table. Emma and Mickey immediately grabbed one, and as soon as Cindy made herself a cup of coffee, she took one as well and settled at her desk.

"So, fill us in on the law firm, Emma. How did it go?" Cindy took a bite of the raspberry-filled donut—it was just as good as she'd imagined.

"It was fine. It's a nice office, actually, as far as temp assignments go. But, I didn't learn a thing. Sheila told me that she and Nancy were best friends, which we already knew. And Justin Powell is a big spender that takes long lunches and likes to drink martinis. How he gets anything done after that is beyond me."

"How do you know he drinks martinis at lunch?" Mickey asked.

"Alyssa, the receptionist told me. And I saw him come back louder than when he left and saw one of their lunch receipts. He always picks up the tab and puts it in as an expense, and I scanned it into the computer. I took a look at it first and they all had several martinis."

"Well, he is a big guy. He probably ate a lot of food too and is used to handling his liquor," Cindy said.

"Maybe he's an alcoholic. One of those functioning ones. I read about that... they drink every day, and can handle a lot more alcohol than most and still get their work done," Mickey said.

"I can't imagine," Cindy said. If she had more than two glasses of wine, she'd feel it the next day and getting any work done after drinking like that would be impossible.

"Have I missed anything? Do we have any new cases?" Emma asked.

"No, you didn't miss anything. It's been slow. Mickey and I both took yesterday off and I just checked messages. We do have some new things to work on, though. We have a reverse alimony situation to investigate. Claire Sturgess is going through a bitter divorce with her dead-beat husband, Owen. He hasn't worked in over twelve years and has spent his time golfing and talking about starting some kind of business. He actually told her that he wants a divorce, which shocked her, and he's demanding 90,000 a year in alimony."

Mickey almost dropped his donut. "Is he out of his mind? He expects her to pay him? Why so much?"

"Claire has basically been the breadwinner since they got married. He quit his job six months later, and she never pushed him to find something because her job pays so well. She's in software sales and is a VP with stock equity and a mid-six figure salary."

"He doesn't work at all?" Emma sounded just as surprised as Mickey.

"Well, now he is. But it's for a start-up, and he's claiming that he has an equity-only arrangement. He won't get anything until the company sells. But Claire thinks he's full of it and once the divorce is final, he'll start taking a salary."

"Won't that change what she has to give him for alimony, then?" Emma asked.

"Yes, but he still might find a way to hide it. Claire doesn't trust him."

"So, what can we do to help?"

"Claire thinks he has a girlfriend and that things are pretty serious. He pretty much admitted it to her and told her that he never loved her. And that he was just biding his time." It had totally disgusted Cindy, and she hoped that they'd be able to help.

"So, he's pretty much a con man then. He deliberately didn't work so that when they got divorced, there'd be a precedent and she'd have to pay him. It doesn't seem fair. I mean, it happens all the time with women, but usually it's because they are taking care of children, not something like this," Emma said.

Cindy nodded. "Right. So, here's what Claire is thinking. If we can get evidence that this girlfriend is staying with Owen, that might help her be able to dismiss the alimony claim or at least get it significantly reduced."

"What do we know about the girlfriend? Have they been together long?" Emma asked.

"Claire's not sure how long they've been seeing each other. She said she's a lot younger though, just twenty-four. Owen is forty-eight."

Emma groaned. "Ugh. What does she see in him?"

Mickey chuckled. "If I had to guess, she probably thinks Owen is the one with the money. Where do they live?"

"You're probably right, Mickey. They have a huge waterfront house on Priscilla Beach. It's on a double lot and they had it custom-built a few years ago. He's twelve years older than Claire too. He likes younger women," Cindy said.

"What are their living arrangements, now?" Emma asked.

"They are taking turns with the house, spending alternate weeks there. Claire has another house, a rental cottage on White Horse Beach that has been in her family for years. So she's spending a lot of time there, but she doesn't want to give up the main house to him. He's supposedly just renting a room at the Pilgrim Sands when he's not there."

"So where do we start?" Emma asked.

"This one will take a while. We'll need several weeks of surveillance to establish a pattern of them being together. If she just sleeps over one night, that's not as strong as if we can show them together more than that. He's at the main house this week and next week he'll be at Pilgrim Sands. Maybe you can go by early morning and watch to see them leave for work. The start-up he's working at is in the industrial park. The morning will be the better proof, I think. But maybe tail him all day today, to see where he goes at lunch too. Could be they meet up then as well."

"I agree. We'll cover all the bases," Mickey said.

"We have a skip-tracing job too. A tenant over at an apartment complex in Kingston up and left owing three months of rent. They want us to find where he went so they can get their money. He's been gone for a month and they haven't been able to track him down."

"That shouldn't be too hard," Mickey said. "There should be a trail by now online."

"Good. I told them we'd try our best." Cindy also warned the property manager that they couldn't guarantee they'd find the missing tenant, and they understood as they'd worked with Fred before.

The front door opened and they all turned in surprise. They weren't expecting anyone. Especially not a policeman. The officer was about Cindy's age, with black hair that was graying around his temples and dark brown eyes. He looked vaguely familiar, but she couldn't place him.

He looked around the office and then held out his hand to Cindy.

"Officer Gregory, Rich Gregory. You must be Cindy, Fred's ex? I'm very sorry for your loss."

Cindy nodded. "Yes, thank you. That's my daughter, Emma, and our associate investigator, Mickey."

The officer smiled and nodded. "I know Mickey. How are you?"

"I'm good, Rich. How're things at the department?"

"Well, that's why I'm stopping by." He glanced at Cindy again. "I used to have a decent working relationship of sorts with Fred. He had cases now and then that we were also working on. We never worked together really, but Fred was good about keeping us in the loop and he was pretty effective, I have to admit. I didn't think that would continue once Fred passed, but I understand that Belinda Russell recently engaged your services?"

"She did. But that was before they found Nancy. She asked us to put our efforts on hold to see how things went with your investigation first," Cindy said.

"Right. So, that's what I wanted to update you on. Figured I'd stop in and let you know that we have this under control. So, you don't need to get involved."

"Does that mean you found who killed Nancy?" Mickey asked quietly. Cindy had never seen him quite so serious. She hoped that was the case and they could wrap things up quickly for Belinda.

"Well, not quite yet. But we're working on it. We have some leads we are chasing. We put a tracer on Nancy's cell phone and the path it took the day after she disappeared might lead us to her killer."

"So, you really have nothing concrete yet though?" Mickey said.

"'I'm sure we will soon. Anyway, just wanted to make sure we are all on the same page here. You all have a good day." Cindy watched Rich leave, feeling irritated. She didn't like being told by anyone what to do. And then it hit her where she knew him from. She wondered if Rich lived in the Pinehills too, as she'd once seen him heading out for a round of golf with Lee's husband and a few others.

"Well, that was annoying. Who does that guy think he is, warning us off?" Emma said indignantly.

"He's usually a good guy. Maybe this being more of a high profile case, he's just letting us know they are on it and don't want us getting in the way," Mickey said as he reached for a second donut.

"Maybe," Cindy said. Before he'd gotten so bossy, she'd been noticing how handsome the officer was. He probably had a wife that didn't work and cooked him dinners every night, though.

"So, Emma do you want to work with Mickey to track down that tenant?" Cindy asked.

"We're on it!" Emma said.

———

LATER THAT NIGHT, EMMA PICKED UP A PIZZA FROM Monte Cristo's on her way home. It was right around the corner on route 3A across from Luke's Liquors and Manomet Point Road, which led down to Taylor Avenue.

She stopped at Luke's Liquors too and picked up some chardonnay as Tess and her daughter, Hayley, were going to walk over and have dinner on the deck with her.

Tess had been over once already, the morning after Emma ran in to her at the gym. She'd brought Hayley then too, and they'd had coffee on the beach while Hayley played in the sand. They'd chatted for several hours and it had gone by so fast. They'd had so much to catch up on, and then it was like no time had passed at all. Emma was thrilled that Tess lived so close by.

She brought the pizza, paper plates and napkins out to the deck and went back in for the wine and glasses, and a root beer for Hayley. She noticed that the bowl of dry cat food she'd left out was almost empty. Her friend, the orange cat, must have been by again. She'd seen him earlier that morning and gave him some food then, too. She'd tested out the name Oscar on him, and he didn't seem to mind. Or maybe he was just hungry. It seemed to fit him, though. As she finished opening the wine, she saw Hayley and Tess walking up from the beach.

"Emma, look what I found!" Hayley was all excited as she ran over to Emma and showed her the pretty blue piece of seaglass she'd found on her walk.

"That's beautiful, Hayley!"

It was a gorgeous night, warm with a slight breeze and still light out. They all ate pizza and Emma and Tess sipped their wine as they chatted and watched the waves crash along the shore and people walking by.

"So, you didn't learn anything on the temp job? I thought that sounded exciting, going undercover," Tess said. Emma had told her about the possible case and swore her to secrecy. She trusted Tess, though. She'd always been good at keeping secrets.

"Not a thing. Except that Justin Powell might have a drinking problem. But that's just my opinion."

Tess laughed. "He's a huge flirt too, you know. I stop into Sushi Joy sometimes for takeout on the way home from the gym and he's always there at the bar, every Thursday by four. He's offered to buy me a drink almost every time, and I always explain that I'm just there getting takeout and have to get home. I felt like asking him where his wife was. You would never know that guy is married."

"I'm not surprised."

"Well, it looks like you two are up to no good," Brady called out as he walked by. "Tess, good to see you." He looked like he'd just gotten off a plane. He was wearing a shirt and tie and carrying an overnight bag and a suit jacket.

"Why don't you come have a drink with us?" Tess called back.

"I'd love to, believe me. But I just got back in town and I'm running late for dinner with my mom. Have to jump in the shower and then meet her downtown at Cafe Strega." He looked Emma's way. "Another time, though. We still need to have that beer and catch up!" He waved goodbye as he stepped inside.

"You still haven't really talked to him yet?" Tess said.

"No, I only ran into him once. We seem to have opposite schedules or maybe he's been traveling, I'm not sure."

"Hmm. Yeah, he does travel a lot," Tess said. "He

comes into the gym when he's here and he told me what he does but I don't really remember, some kind of consulting, lots of flying to different towns for the week, home on Friday kind of thing."

"Does he have a girlfriend?" Emma asked.

Tess raised her eyebrows. "Are you interested?"

"No. Just curious. I knew him years ago, but we lost touch. I always remembered he was a good guy though and fun. We were never single at the same time. So, I doubt we are now, either. Just the way it goes."

"Hmm. He hasn't mentioned anyone in a while. Not that he ever really did, but sometimes I'd see him around town with someone, or working out together in the gym." She took a sip of wine and looked deep in thought for a moment. "Actually, now that I think of it. The last person I remember seeing him hanging out with at the gym, was Nancy."

"That Nancy?" Emma set her wine glass down.

"Yeah. She was a few years older than him. I just assumed they were friends, workout buddies. They met up almost every week for several months, usually Tuesday or Wednesday mornings, and they came in together and left together. I didn't think much of it at the time."

"That's interesting. Maybe they were just workout buddies. He wasn't mentioned as one of her exes. We had a few other guys on the list that her best friend Sheila gave us."

"Well, a best friend would know, right?" Tess picked up the bottle of wine and added a splash to her glass. She held it over Emma's and Emma nodded.

"Yes, I'll take a bit more wine, thanks." She took a sip after Tess filled her glass, and they both waved at Brady as he walked out of his cottage toward his car. She watched him drive off and wondered just how well he'd known Nancy.

CHAPTER 10

"Remember, head down and arms straight. One more basket of balls, ladies, and then we'll call it a day," Rob said. He was their golf instructor. Rachel had been trying to get them to take golf lessons together for ages. Finally, Lee and Cindy agreed to take a ladies eight-week beginners clinic with her.

The class took place on Saturday morning and they spent the first day on the driving range, learning how to hit properly. Cindy had always been a little intimidated by golf, even though living in the Pinehills they had access to one of the nicest courses in Plymouth.

"When we finish the course, we can join the ladies golf league. They play every Tuesday night and have dinner at East Bay after," Rachel said.

Cindy and Lee exchanged glances.

"I think Cindy and I are a long way away from league level," Lee said.

"Someone told me they take all levels. Everyone has a

handicap based on their skill level, so it doesn't matter. It's as much a social thing as anything else," Rachel said.

"Why are you so keen on this, Rachel?" Cindy asked and noticed with interest that Rachel's face flushed.

"I know why! She thinks it might be a good way to meet men," Lee said.

That hadn't even occurred to Cindy.

"Really? Is that why, Rachel? You've never shown any interest in golf until recently."

Rachel sighed. "Okay, that's true, sort of. But, I do think it might a fun thing for us, too. We've lived here for ages and aside from the two of you, I don't know anyone else in the Pinehills, do you?"

"Not really," Cindy admitted.

"I know a few of Bob's friends, but other than that, no. I suppose you're right. It might be good for us. Good exercise too," Lee agreed.

And so they'd signed up for the classes. They met at the driving range at nine and finished up a few minutes before noon.

"Anyone up for lunch at East Bay?" Rachel asked.

Cindy and Lee quickly agreed, and they made their way over to the restaurant which was located at the golf club, and were seated outside. It was a pretty spot. The food was consistently good. Cindy and Lee ordered the steak tips over Caesar salad, and Rachel ordered a burger.

They sipped iced tea and caught up on each other's week while they ate. For dessert they decided to share a slice of cheesecake and linger for a bit over coffee. As they were finishing up, Cindy turned at the sound of a familiar voice. Lee's husband, Bob, called out hello as he walked by on his way to get a golf cart. He was with three others, and one of them was Rich, the cop that had stopped by the agency.

"Has Bob known that guy Rich long?" Cindy asked.

"Rich Gregory?"

Cindy nodded.

Lee thought for a moment. "Not too long. I think he moved into the Pinehills maybe six months ago? He plays in the golf league with Bob. Seems like a nice enough guy. Why do you ask?"

"Just curious. He stopped by the office the other day, introduced himself and basically told us to keep away from his case."

"The Nancy case?" Rachel asked.

"Yes. He said they have a few leads and have it under control. He seemed afraid that we might screw things up."

Lee laughed. "He might have a point. No offense meant."

Cindy laughed too. "Well, true. But he was a little annoying about it. I mean, Emma and I are new at this, but Mickey's not."

"Yeah, but Mickey's not exactly a spring chicken. Maybe Rich thinks he is too old to be effective."

"Maybe he's afraid you all might make him look bad?" Rachel offered.

"That's sweet of you to say, but I think Lee's answer is

probably closer to the truth. It just irritated me. He warned us off and none of us liked that."

"So, what are you going to do?" Lee asked.

"Nothing, yet. We're sort of on pause with the case until Belinda gives us the green light. She might never do that, if the police wrap this up soon."

"It doesn't sound like they are close, based on what I've been reading. They just keep saying everyone they talk to says Nancy was well-liked. No one can imagine anyone wanting to hurt her. Maybe it was a random killing? That's a scary thought," Rachel said.

"It's possible, but unlikely," Cindy said. "I've been reading up a lot lately on murder investigations, and random killings are actually very rare. It's almost always someone known to the victim."

"Do you guys have any theories on who it could be?" Lee asked.

Cindy shook her head. "No. No idea. We'd only just begun to question people when she was found and we put the investigation on hold. Mickey says if we talk to enough people, eventually we'll find our way to the truth. I like his optimism, but it seems hard to believe. If the police can't find the person, how likely is it that we will?" Cindy kept going back and forth about that in her mind. She was excited about the possibility that they might solve this case, but it also just seemed unlikely if the police couldn't find the killer.

"I think he might be single, you know," Lee said as she waved to Bob and Rich as they drove by in their golf cart.

"Really? What do you know about him?" Rachel asked.

For some reason, Cindy found her interest annoying. "I don't think he's your type."

"Since when is tall, dark and handsome not my type?" Rachel said with a smile.

"He's a cop. Works with Andy." Rachel had dated the police officer for a few months when she first joined a dating service and he was so controlling that she made Lee and Cindy promise to stop her from dating a cop ever again.

"Oh, right. I did say that. Never mind then. Maybe you should go for him, Cindy."

"Yes, are you interested, Cindy? I could make an introduction happen?" Lee seemed excited by the idea.

Cindy instantly regretted saying anything. "No, I'm not interested, at all. Even if I was, it probably wouldn't be a good idea to date him of all people. I mean, if we end up getting involved in the investigation."

Lee looked amused. "Right, probably not a good idea at all. Still, maybe I will have an appetizer party soon and invite our new neighbor. As a cop, he might be a good friend to have."

"HEY, OSCAR." EMMA WAS SITTING ON HER DECK, drinking her morning coffee and eating her oatmeal and banana when the orange cat was suddenly there again, rubbing against her leg, and purring. She took her last bite of oatmeal, then scooped the cat into her lap. This was their new routine. He came by every morning and sat for two minutes in Emma's lap, enjoyed a good scratching behind the ears, and then he was ready for his breakfast.

Sure enough, after exactly two minutes, he jumped down and padded over to the bowl of dry food that was waiting for him by the front door. There was one of fresh water too. He ate his fill and then plopped down in a sunny spot on the deck and went to sleep. Emma knew he'd snooze for a while, then be on his way. She still wasn't sure what his situation was, but she was starting to think he was a homeless kitty as he came every morning and ate quite a bit. She'd already had to pick up a second box of food. She only saw him in the morning, though. So, maybe he did have a home, or someone else fed him in the evening. At the moment, sound asleep with the breeze ruffling the fur on his belly, he looked quite content.

Emma showered and headed off to drive by Owen's house on her way into the office. They were in their second week now of watching Claire's deadbeat husband, Owen. Their efforts so far had been disappointing. When they'd gone by every morning so far, there hadn't been any other cars in the driveway other than Owen's. But her mother said that Claire called in and gave the update that she overheard Owen on the phone making plans to see his girlfriend, Amber, today and that she'd been out of town at a conference. So, they were hopeful they might actually see something useful soon.

Emma was the first one into the office and had told

Mickey the day before that she was bringing lunch for them. She'd made healthy turkey sandwiches on whole wheat bread and had baby carrots to snack on. She and Mickey were developing bad habits between donuts in the morning and potato chips in the afternoon. He agreed that they needed to do better, and they'd quit it on the junk food for a while.

Her mother and Mickey walked in at the same time.

"Did you check the email yet, honey?" her mother asked.

Emma nodded. "I'm looking at it now. We have two more workman's comp cases coming this week, and there's a note from Belinda Russell asking you to give her a call. Maybe there's news on her case?"

"Maybe. Hopefully. I'll call her now." Her mother made herself a quick cup of coffee first, then settled at her desk and called Belinda, but had to leave a voice message.

"I'll update you guys when I connect with her. Good luck today."

"Thanks, we'll see you later."

"I'll be out mid-day at the yoga studio, but I'll be checking messages and will be back later this afternoon."

Emma and Mickey headed out and Emma noticed Mickey was carrying a big brown paper bag.

"What's that?" she asked as she buckled her seatbelt.

Mickey finished buckling in and then opened the bag as Emma backed out of the lot. "So, I stopped at Clement's this morning and I was going to get us a couple of healthy bran muffins. But they were just putting out a fresh batch of apple-filled jelly donuts."

"I thought we agreed no more donuts?"

Mickey grinned. "I couldn't resist. They're still warm. Try one." He handed a donut to Emma, and he was right. They were still warm.

"You're a bad influence," Emma teased him.

"So I've been told."

Emma drove to Owen's office building in the industrial park. They parked as usual, in the lot as far away as possible but close enough to still see people coming and going out the front door. Owen's routine so far hadn't been very interesting. He usually went out at lunch time, but typically just grabbed a sandwich or fast food and brought it back to his office.

But today, they followed him to the Plymouth and Brockton bus station behind McDonald's at the exit five rest area. As it was the middle of the day, they doubted he was taking the bus to Boston.

"Maybe the girlfriend's flight came in and she took the bus from Logan?" Mickey said.

So far, they hadn't had a glimpse of this supposed girlfriend, so Emma hoped he was right but was beginning to wonder if she existed.

Five minutes after they arrived, the bus arrived, and they watched as passengers disembarked. Owen got out of his car and walked over to the front of the bus. He was definitely waiting for someone.

And then they saw her. A pretty, blond-haired woman ran over to Owen and jumped into his arms, wrapping her legs around him. He seemed startled and for a moment Emma wondered if he was going to topple over, but he managed to hang on and hugged her back hard. And a moment later there was no doubt that Owen indeed had a girlfriend as the two shared a long, deep kiss.

They watched as Owen grabbed her suitcase, put the luggage in the back seat of his car and they drove off.

Emma followed carefully. She was starting to feel like a pro at keeping just the right distance. Fifteen minutes later, they arrived outside Owen and Claire's house in Priscilla Beach. Owen grabbed the girl's suitcase and they kissed again before heading into the house. Mickey took several pictures, both at the bus station and outside the house.

"So now what?" Emma asked.

"We wait a bit, see if he goes back to work. Then we'll head into the office. It's a little trickier with her not having a car. Seems like she's not from around here then."

"Maybe they met online? One of those dating sites?" Emma suggested.

"Could be. I don't know much about that," Mickey admitted.

"People meet online from all across the country. Or could be she met him when she was in town once before, maybe she was here on business or vacation."

"If she stays with him all week and we can get evidence of that, it could really help Claire's case," Mickey said.

"So, maybe tomorrow we come here earlier and see if

we can get a shot of her kissing him goodbye as he heads off to work," Emma said.

"I like the way you think. That sounds like a good plan."

They followed Owen back to the office and decided there wasn't anything further to be gained that day by following him, so they called it quits early. They stopped back at the office and Mickey was going to head home, but when they saw Emma's mother's car in the parking lot, they decided to go inside for a minute and fill her in.

Once they brought her up to speed, Emma's mother shocked them with an update of her own.

"So, I connected with Belinda, and she wants us to start working on Nancy's case again."

CHAPTER 11

Since Emma went home early and it was a beautiful day, she decided to walk the beach. She changed into sweats and sneakers, pulled her hair in a ponytail and put her headphones on so she could listen to Pandora radio as she walked. Because it was such a nice day, the beach was busy with people walking and quite a few had beach chairs and towels even though it wasn't really that warm yet. Not for bathing suits, but for sitting and chatting while wearing sweatshirts, absolutely.

Emma walked the length of the beach in both directions and about thirty minutes later, she was done and stretching on her deck. It was almost five by then and she could feel a slight shift in the air, a temperature drop as evening approached.

She was staring out at the ocean, thinking about Nancy's case and how they'd begin working on it the next day, when a voice interrupted her thoughts.

"How do you feel about lobster?" Brady asked. He'd

walked over and looked like he'd been exercising too, maybe just returned from the gym as he was in sweats and a baseball cap.

"I like lobster. But then everyone does, right?"

He laughed. "My mother won't touch it. I was thinking of putting an order in with the Lobster Pound. They'll steam them for us. I figure I'll place the order—for two lobsters, if you want to join me. Then I'll jump in the shower and by the time I'm done, they'll be ready." The Lobster Pound was a seafood market right around the corner at the very tip of Manomet Point Road. It had the best view around and in Emma's opinion, kind of wasted on a seafood market, but it was convenient when you wanted lobster.

"That sounds great. I haven't had lobster since I've been home."

"Perfect. We can eat on your deck and catch up. I have beer I can bring over too?"

"Just bring what you want to drink. I've got wine. I have some potato salad too, we can have that with the lobster."

"Awesome."

Forty-five minutes later, Brady knocked on Emma's back door. He was carrying a styrofoam container that held the steamed lobsters with one hand, and had a six-pack of beer in the other. Emma had big plates for them and a bowl for their shells. She'd also cut up a lemon and melted some butter for dipping. They brought everything out to the deck and sat at Emma's picnic table. It was the perfect night for it. The air was still and just warm enough that they could sit outside comfortably in their sweatshirts.

The lobster was delicious. They both wore the plastic bibs so that they wouldn't spray water and lobster fat on themselves when they cracked the claws open.

"So, Emma, tell me what you've been up to all these years. I heard you went to Hollywood. Did you meet anyone famous?"

She laughed. "I did meet some famous people." She mentioned a few names, and he was suitably impressed.

"So, you had a good time there. Do you miss it?"

Did she? She was surprised by how little she missed Hollywood now that she was back home. Hollywood had never felt like home. It was just where she lived for a while.

"I really don't. I thought that I would. I'm glad I went there and tried it, though."

"I always thought you were so talented. I remember seeing you in some school musicals."

She smiled, remembering how much fun she'd had performing in those high school shows.

"Thanks. That feels like another lifetime," she admitted.

"What are you doing for work now?" he asked.

"My mother and I took over my dad's private investigator business, along with Mickey who worked for him for years."

Brady looked surprised. "No kidding? What's that like? Is it as exciting as they show on TV?"

Emma laughed. "I don't think exciting is quite the

word. Not always. I like it though." She told him about some of the surveillance work that she and Mickey had done so far.

"That sounds pretty cool, actually."

"Well, it's interesting when something happens. There's a lot of sitting around waiting. That can be a little boring."

"Every job has its downsides," Brady said as he dunked a chunk of claw meat in the melted butter.

"What do you do for work? It seems like you travel a lot."

"I do. I'm a software consultant and I go where the clients are. Some work can be done remotely, but not always and never when a job first starts. I need to meet people face to face and figure out what they are trying to do and then get it implemented." He seemed full of energy as he spoke, and Emma sensed that he enjoyed his work.

"You love what you do," she said.

He grinned. "Yeah, I do. Aside from the travel, it's a pretty cool job."

"Tess said you work out at our gym too?"

"You go to Plymouth Fitness? Yeah, when I'm in town I get there as often as I can. Usually early morning."

"I'm not a morning person when it comes to the gym. I do classes after work sometimes and usually get there on the weekends. Unless the weather is like today and then I'll just get a good walk in."

Brady glanced out at the beach, which was still busy

with people walking even though the sun was going down. It was still so nice out.

"Yeah, it's pretty sweet here. I try to hit the beach on the weekends if I'm in town. I go through spurts where I'm not traveling and then I'll sneak out in the afternoon sometimes for an hour or so and just soak in the sun."

Emma tried to think of a way to ask him about Nancy.

Finally, she just brought it up. "I was reading the local news earlier and they still haven't found anything on whoever killed Nancy Eldridge. Crazy to think something like that could happen here in Plymouth. Did you know her?" She said it casually.

"Yeah, I did know Nancy. Damn shame what happened. Can't imagine who would do that. She was a good girl. Everyone loved her."

"You knew her? That's what I read too. No one has any idea and everyone liked her. So they don't have any solid leads. Maybe it was a random thing?"

Brady frowned. "Maybe, though, that kind of thing doesn't happen in Plymouth. I mean never has as far as I know. It's not like it's Boston, you know?"

Emma nodded in agreement.

They were both quiet for a moment and then Brady cracked open a claw and had a few bites. He looked deep in thought before saying, "We worked out together sometimes. I actually called her the day after she disappeared to see if she wanted to go to the gym with me, but she never answered. Of course, I didn't know then that she was gone."

"Did you know her well? Any idea if she was dating anyone?"

"I knew her pretty well. We actually went on a date about six months ago, I met her on one of those dating sites. She's a great girl, but there was just no chemistry there. She felt the same way. I actually would have gone out a second time, but she shut that down. But she said we could be friends and that she needed a workout buddy to keep her accountable. It stung for about two seconds, but she was right."

"So she probably didn't talk to you about her dating life then?" Emma wondered if that would be weird to have that conversation with someone that you'd dated.

"Oh no, she did. After our one date, we shifted gears pretty quickly and developed a good friendship. She dated two other guys in the last two months, but they didn't last long either. She worked long hours and said it was always hard on relationships."

"You had that in common, with your travel," Emma said.

He grinned. "We did. That's why we went on the first date. It seemed like we had a lot in common. Chemistry is a funny thing, though. It's either there or it's not. You can't really force it. I liked her enough to go on a second date, but I was more relieved than anything when she said she wasn't feeling it. Dating can be hard."

"That is so true," Emma agreed.

"So, what's your story, Emma. Are you dating anyone?"

"No. I haven't been back long and really haven't gone

out much since I've been home. I went to Su Casa with my brother and his girlfriend a few weeks ago, that's about it."

Brady smiled. "Well, I'm sure it won't take you long, once you do get out there. I actually love Su Casa. We should go there sometime."

"Sure. I owe you, since you treated me to lobster tonight."

"No, you don't. It was nothing. I was ordering one anyway. I'm glad we caught up though. We have to do this again soon."

Brady helped her clean up and put all the lobster remnants in the trash. He insisted on taking the garbage bag with him.

"I'm going to the dump tomorrow. This will stink your place up otherwise."

"Thanks. This was fun. Thanks again for the lobster."

He smiled. A slow, lazy grin that made her notice how green his eyes were. She shivered as a sudden gust of cool air took her by surprise and the wind made the kitchen door slam shut.

CHAPTER 12

Belinda Russell came by the office the next morning around ten to fill them in on where the police stood with the investigation of Nancy's murder. Because they were having company, Cindy picked up a box of donuts. Belinda declined the sugary treat and just had a black coffee. Meanwhile, Mickey's eyes lit up when Cindy opened the cardboard box and the sweet scent of the donuts filled the room. He and Emma both helped themselves, jelly-filled for Mickey and glazed with pink sprinkles for Emma. Once they were all settled around the coffee table, Cindy began the meeting.

"Thank you for taking the time to stop in. Anything you can share about what the police have done and discovered would be helpful," she said.

Emma set her donut down, picked up a pen and opened her notebook.

"So, they say they've talked to everyone they can

possibly think of. And there's only one person that is even remotely close to being a suspect," Belinda said.

Mickey leaned forward. "Who's that?"

They'd all been following the case closely, but there had been little revealed in the papers so far.

"Well, I think it's ridiculous, and it's part of the reason I want you all to get going on this again. They seem to have honed in on one person and aren't really looking at anyone else now. I'm just worried that they are going down the wrong path and will miss catching the real killer."

"Who do they think it might be?" Cindy asked.

"Peter Johnson. Sheila Johnson's husband, or rather ex-husband. Sheila is the office manager at the law firm where Nancy works and she handled the divorce for Sheila."

"Why do they think it's him? Did he and Nancy not get along?" Emma asked.

"It doesn't make any sense to me. He hardly knew Nancy, just through Sheila when they were going through the divorce. It wasn't amicable, and Sheila only talks to him now about the kids. They have shared custody. So, Nancy only saw him a few times, and not for long."

"Did he say something to the police that was incriminating?" Cindy asked.

"They talked to him, but didn't get anything. They weren't really even counting him as a suspect until they got the results back from cell phone tracking. There were no messages that were significant, but whoever took Nancy, took her cell phone too and didn't get rid of it right away. It looks like whoever killed her then drove to the Kingston commuter train lot and took the train to Boston. The signal stopped there. They think the killer realized they needed to get rid of Nancy's phone and disposed of it when they reached South Station."

"So, how does that make the police think it might be Peter? I thought I read that everyone they've talked to so far had an alibi," Cindy asked.

Belinda nodded. "They did. But Peter's alibi was that he was working, and his job is as a train conductor. He says his shift was split, which they say is common with conductors. He started at noon, had a four-hour break in the late afternoon, and then was back on at eight and finished up around midnight. It's the same route that the phone showed, with all the stops. They said his break would have given him time to kill Nancy, dispose of her body and go back to work."

"It really is amazing that they can track cell phones that way," Cindy said. "But you're not convinced?"

Belinda shook her head. "Not yet. I suppose it's possible, but I think it's a bit of a reach. It could have been anyone that took the train to Boston and disposed of her phone when they got there. They don't really have anything else on him."

"No DNA in his car?" Mickey asked.

"No, nothing," Belinda confirmed.

"Still, he's a conductor on the commuter route. The timing of it is interesting," Emma said.

"It might be him. I'm not ruling him out. I just don't want the search to stop with him," Belinda said. "It doesn't make sense to me that Peter would hurt Nancy. Unless there are things we don't know. I don't really know her friend Sheila very well. She and Nancy only grew close this past year."

"Okay, if you learn anything else that you think we should know, please keep us posted," Cindy said.

"We'll get started right away on this. I'll see if we can talk to that Peter guy as soon as possible. And we'll do our own investigation and talk to everyone else the police have already talked to," Mickey assured her.

Belinda looked relieved. "Thank you. That's all I want, just a thorough investigation of every possible suspect. Not a rush to convict someone before we are sure."

"We will give you updates as soon as we have any news at all," Cindy promised.

Belinda stood and took the last sip of her coffee. "I appreciate your time. I look forward to hearing your updates."

Cindy walked her to the door and promised to be in touch as soon as possible. Once Belinda was gone, Cindy added a splash of coffee to her mug as well as Emma and Mickey's and they settled back down to make a plan. Cindy suddenly felt hungry and reached for a donut. She needed energy after all, and who was she kidding—the glazed with sprinkles was her favorite, too.

"So, what do you both make of that?" Cindy asked. "Interesting about the cell phone tracking, isn't it?"

Mickey nodded. "They can do more and more with technology. Pretty soon they won't need us at all!"

Emma laughed. "It is cool what they can do now, but they will always need people involved. I think a lot of what we do is intuitive, especially when you talk to someone and get a feeling about how truthful they are."

"Who will you talk to first?" Cindy asked.

Mickey chuckled. "Whoever answers the phone and agrees to meet with us. But Peter will be the first person I call."

"What if he doesn't want to talk to you? No one has to talk to us, right?" Cindy said.

"That's true, but most people can't resist talking, whether it's to clear their name or to convince you that they aren't guilty. So, innocent or not, they usually agree to a chat. Sometimes they don't say yes right away, and I have to pour on the Mickey charm and give them a second or a third chance." He grinned. "They usually come around."

"There's another person we might want to add to our list," Emma said. "I don't think it's anything, but my next-door neighbor, Brady Smith, knew Nancy pretty well too. My friend, Tess, who is a trainer at the gym, told me he and Nancy were workout buddies, and maybe more. She said they used to come in together several times a week before work."

"I remember Brady. Did you ask him about it? He was very handsome, if I remember. Dark blond hair?" Cindy asked.

Emma nodded. "Yep, that's Brady. He's actually better-looking now. We chatted the other night, and it came up in conversation. He shared that they actually dated, but just once, and realized they were better as friends. So, I don't think there's anything there."

Mickey didn't look as convinced. "We'll have another chat with Mr. Brady. I'll question him and see if his story matches what he told you. Not to scare either of you, but Ted Bundy was a handsome, charming fellow too."

EMMA SUPPOSED THAT MICKEY WAS RIGHT AND THEY should do a more formal interview with Brady. Because she knew him, she agreed to make the call to ask if they could come out for a chat. Mickey had already called Peter, and he agreed to talk to them but wasn't available until the end of the week. Emma knew that Brady wasn't traveling this week, as she'd seen him heading out to the gym that morning.

He answered on the first ring and sounded amused when she asked if she and Mickey could come out and talk to him about Nancy.

"Sure, I have nothing to hide. Happy to help. I'm working at home all week. Swing by this afternoon if you like."

"Will do. Thanks, Brady." She ended the call and turned to Mickey, who was openly eavesdropping.

"What did he say?"

"He said he'd be happy to chat with us. We can stop by this afternoon."

"Excellent."

Mickey got through to Sheila at the law office and she

agreed to meet with him Friday afternoon and also scheduled fifteen minutes for him to speak with Justin, too.

"It's probably best if I go alone, since you temped
there and all," Mickey said.

Emma nodded. "Right. Rachel said there might be
another assignment coming up either this week or next.
Just a few days, so that might be a good idea, too."

"Can't hurt. Especially if it does turn out to be
Sheila's husband—you might pick up something that they
don't reveal in my conversation. Maybe you should
suggest after-work drinks one day," Mickey suggested. "A
little liquor loosens lips. Or so they say."

"Are you speaking from experience?" Emma laughed.

"Well, not personal experience. I don't ever have
more than one drink. But more than once I've had
conversations in bars with subjects, and once they have a
few drinks, they sometimes share quite a bit."

"Maybe I should pick up a six-pack of beer on the
way to Brady's?" Emma joked.

"Not a bad idea, if it wasn't early afternoon," Mickey
agreed.

After a quick lunch, Emma's mother headed off to
teach an afternoon yoga class and Mickey and Emma
went to visit Brady.

White Horse Beach was quiet when they walked
down the long wooden walkway along the sand that led to
their cottages. It was a Tuesday, and everyone was at
work. Mid-May was still too early in the season to be very
busy with tourists. They parked in Emma's parking spot
in the lot just off the street, and Emma noticed that

Brady's car was there too. When they reached his cottage, his back door was open a crack and Emma saw Oscar saunter by. He glanced at them, twitched his tail and turned toward the beach. Emma wondered if he'd just left Brady's house. Maybe he was Brady's cat.

Mickey knocked on the door and they waited. A moment later, a voice hollered for them to come in. Emma opened the door and stepped inside. Brady's cottage was a mirror image of hers. It was the same layout and size, just decorated differently. Where Emma's was all light, beachy colors and lots of white, Brady's was much darker. His hardwood floors were deep brown, there was hunter green trim on the windows, and black granite counters in the small kitchen.

They walked through the living room to Brady's deck, where he was sitting at a table with an umbrella and had two laptops in front of him and his cell phone in the middle. The living room was also dark, with chocolate brown leather furniture and charcoal-colored bookcases lining one wall. The whole cottage had a very masculine, somewhat cold feel. There was nothing out of place, no clutter anywhere. It almost looked like no one lived there. Though, Emma supposed with all his traveling, Brady wasn't around much to mess it up.

"Hey, sorry I didn't come greet you. I was just finishing up a call." He stood and held out his hand, and Mickey shook it. "I'm all yours. Have a seat. Can I get you anything? Coffee, water?"

"I'm good, thanks," Mickey said.

"I'm fine, too. Thanks, Brady," Emma said.

They settled across from Brady at the round, wooden table and he returned to his seat.

"So, you guys are back on the case. Does that mean the police haven't come up with anything?" Brady asked.

Emma opened her mouth to speak and give him the update that they knew, but Mickey beat her to it, and didn't share much with Brady at all.

"They haven't really found anything, yet. Belinda, Nancy's mother, said the police told her that everyone they've talked to had an alibi. So, we're just starting from scratch and talking to everyone again, to see if there's anything we can find out. Did you talk to the police already?"

Brady shook his head. "No, they never contacted me."

"Sheila, Nancy's best friend, gave the police a list of people that Nancy dated. But your name wasn't there. Should it have been? Emma mentioned that you told her you dated Nancy."

Brady smiled, that easy slow grin as he glanced at Emma. "Yeah, I did mention that to Emma. Nancy and I didn't really date, though. That's probably why Sheila didn't mention it. We went on one date. Then realized we were better as friends. And we both liked to work out and had similar schedules."

Mickey smiled and leaned back. "Who realized it first?" he asked casually.

"Oh, Nancy did. Like I told Emma, I would have gone out with her again, given it a shot, but we really didn't have that kind of chemistry. I enjoyed her company though."

"So, you weren't upset then, or hurt?"

Brady chuckled. "Not at all. She actually made it easy for me. It probably wouldn't have worked. So, she was right. She was the one that suggested we be workout buddies. I had to drive right by her house on the way to gym, so it was her way of being accountable. She needed that extra push to make sure she got to the gym."

"And you didn't?"

"Not really. I'm pretty disciplined about things. I get to the gym at least four or five times a week. It's a great stress reliever."

"I've heard that too. Maybe I should give it a try." They all laughed at that. But then Mickey added, "Are you under a lot of stress? Work-related or otherwise?"

Brady glanced out at the ocean for a moment before answering. "Isn't everyone? I like my job, but it has its moments. I'm the one that hears it when the technology that I implemented doesn't work. It's usually not an issue, but when something goes wrong, it can be big. That's when I'll have to drop everything and fly across the country to wherever the client is and make sure everything gets fixed, ASAP."

"That does sound stressful," Mickey agreed. "Were you even around the night Nancy went missing? Emma says you travel a lot."

"I do. In spurts. This is a good week. I don't have any travel scheduled until late next week. The night Nancy went missing, I think I was in Colorado. That was a big project."

"Did Nancy ever talk to you about her personal life? Anyone she felt threatened by?" Mickey asked.

"We talked some. I knew about the last two guys she dated before she died. But she never said much about either of them. They were kind of vanilla, not memorable, if you know what I mean? It didn't last long with either of them. Nancy worked long hours, like I do. That can be hard. But she was on good terms with both of them. Really with everyone."

"So, she never mentioned being at odds with anyone?"

Brady shook his head. "No, never. Our conversations were never that deep. We chatted about easy stuff, working out, restaurants we liked. I really don't even know who else she hung out with, other than Sheila. They used to have drinks after work sometimes. I don't think Nancy had much of a social life."

"Okay, that's very helpful. Is there anything else you can think of that we should know?"

"That's all I know. Have you talked to Sheila yet?"

"No, not yet. We're talking on Friday."

"Good. Sheila's the one to really pump for information. She knew Nancy better than just about anyone. At least that's the impression I got from Nancy. I never actually met Sheila."

Mickey stood and glanced at Emma and she stood too.

"Well, we won't take up anymore of your time. Thank you for meeting with us."

"My pleasure. I'll walk you guys out."

Emma remembered that she meant to ask Brady something.

"Brady, do you have a cat, by any chance? I noticed an orange cat by your back door when we arrived. And it's been visiting me every morning."

"No, I don't have a cat. I've seen that one around too. It's probably a stray. It's not all that safe for stray animals around here, though. Too many coyotes. I've seen them run along the beach now and then in the early hours or late night. Probably why we don't see too many cats."

"Probably so," Emma had forgotten that coyotes were sometimes an issue. She decided it might be time to invite Oscar inside.

CHAPTER 13

The rest of the week flew by, and before Cindy knew it, Friday had arrived. Originally, Emma and Mickey were going to be meeting with Peter, Sheila's ex-husband that morning, but Rachel had called earlier in the week and said that Sheila specifically had requested Emma if she was available to come in that Thursday and Friday. So, while Emma was at the law office, Cindy assumed that Mickey would go alone. But he had a different idea.

"I think you should come with me," he suggested as they sat drinking coffee in the office Friday morning. Cindy had brought in some fresh cut fruit, and while Mickey probably would have preferred a donut, he happily took some cantaloupe.

"Me? What would you want me there for?"

"I think it will be good for you, and for me. It's good to have another set of ears. You can listen and take notes while I chat with Peter. It might be interesting for you, too."

"I don't know." It very much felt out of Cindy's comfort zone. Yet, she was a little intrigued at the same time.

"What else do you have to do? You don't have a class until later this afternoon, right? We're seeing him at eleven and will be done by noon. Might be fun."

"Okay, I'll do it!" Cindy grabbed a notebook and two pens in case one ran out of ink. She slipped both into her tote bag and followed Mickey to his convertible.

"Do you want me to drive?" she offered. Mickey's car was adorable, but small and it was a little windy.

"No, I'll drive. You might want to just tie your hair back, though."

She did as suggested, pulling her hair into a ponytail and securing it with a hair band she kept in her tote and used for her yoga classes.

She climbed into the car. It was low to the ground, but comfortable. Once they were buckled in, Mickey backed out of the lot and headed up Samoset Street and turned onto Route 3, the highway that led to either Boston or Cape Cod. They headed toward the Cape and went four exits down to the most southern Plymouth exit. They were going to a condo at White Cliffs, where Peter lived.

Soon after they merged onto the highway, Mickey stepped on the gas and the car kicked into gear.

"She's got some nice power, huh?" Mickey said proudly.

"Very impressive," Cindy agreed. It was a smooth-riding car, and it was fun to ride along with the top down, feeling the wind in her hair. She felt young and carefree and she could see why Mickey liked the car so much.

Less than twenty minutes later, they pulled up to the gate at White Cliffs, a private condo and golf community. Mickey had to announce who they were there to see and then the gate lifted and they drove in and found Peter's unit and parked in a visitor spot.

Mickey led the way to the front door and a moment later it opened and Peter invited them inside. Cindy was surprised to see that he was quite a bit older than Sheila, who she knew was around forty, like Nancy. Peter looked to be in his mid to late fifties. He seemed a little uncomfortable as he invited them to sit at the kitchen table. She tried to put herself in his shoes though, as this wasn't exactly a social call. And while they weren't the police, they were still talking to him to investigate Nancy's murder, and he was a suspect.

He was average height and weight, medium brown hair, slight pot belly. He looked like most men his age, Cindy's age. He wasn't someone that would stand out in a crowd.

Mickey thanked him for making the time to see them, introduced Cindy and explained again that they were private detectives, hired by Nancy's mother.

"I know you've already talked to the police. We're just doing our due diligence, so I apologize in advance if it feels like you are repeating yourself. It's all new to us though, and we're talking to everyone that Nancy knew to try to piece things together."

"I understand. I want to be helpful and get to the bottom of this too. I can't imagine who would want to hurt that girl."

"You knew her then? Nancy? I know she was a friend of your ex-wife, Sheila."

Peter nodded. "I knew who she was, of course. But I didn't really know her. I think I met her twice, when I was in the office and in court to finalize our divorce. I just know what Sheila told me. She thought the world of Nancy."

"So you didn't see her at all the day she went missing?" Mickey asked casually.

Peter shook his head. "No. I never saw her that day. I was working for one thing and it was a split day, so I had about a four-hour window in the middle of my shift. I did some grocery shopping and ran some errands. Then went back to work until about midnight, when the last train left Boston and arrived in Kingston. I told the police the same thing."

"Right," Mickey agreed. "What about your ex-wife, Sheila? Did she mention anything about this to you? Have any ideas at all what might have happened to Nancy or who she might have been with?"

Peter shook his head. "No. She didn't talk about that at all with me. Sheila and I, well we don't really talk much, other than about picking up the kids."

"Divorces are tough, huh? Nancy handled the divorce for your wife, I think?"

"She did," Peter agreed.

"No resentment there, toward Sheila, or maybe even Nancy? I heard she was a pretty tough lawyer and divorce can be expensive."

Cindy noticed a muscle flex in Peter's jaw. He looked down and away before answering the question.

"It wasn't an easy time for us. There was bitterness, but it was between me and Sheila. It had nothing to do with Nancy. She was just doing her job." He sighed. "And you're right. She was very good at it. But I have no idea who might have done this to her. None at all. I told the police the same thing."

"Very good. I think we're done here then. I do appreciate your time." Mickey fished a business card out of his wallet and handed it to Peter. "If you think of anything else, anything at all, please give me a call. I'd appreciate it."

Peter glanced at the card, then picked it up and stuck it into his wallet. "I'll do that."

Mickey stood, "Alrighty then. We'll let you get back to your day. Thanks again."

When they were buckled in the car and ready to go, Mickey turned to Cindy and asked, "So, what did you think? Is he our guy?"

Cindy shook her head. "I don't know for sure, but I don't think so. He seems a bit lost, and sad, but I can't picture him killing Nancy. He doesn't really seem to have a motive."

"No, he doesn't, does he? At least not one that we

know of, anyway." Mickey grinned. "So, are you glad you came? That was fun, right?"

Cindy laughed. "I don't know that I'd use the word fun, but yes, I'm glad I came. It was very interesting."

"I knew you'd like it."

———

FRIDAY AT NOON, EMMA HAD JUST WALKED OUT FRONT TO cover the reception desk for Alyssa's lunch break when a familiar face walked through the door of the law firm. Mickey was there for his meeting with Sheila and then Justin.

He winked at Emma and she laughed as she called Sheila to let her know Mickey was there.

"She'll be right with you."

"Excellent." Mickey walked around the lobby looking at the photographs of Justin with various famous people. Sheila came out a moment later, and they went back to her office. Emma wished she was a fly on the wall to listen in on that conversation, especially the one with Justin. He was only scheduled to spend fifteen minutes with Mickey, but it went longer and almost an hour later, Justin walked Mickey out and slapped him lightly on the back like they were old friends. They were both laughing and looked like they were having a great time. Mickey left and Justin turned to go back to his office. He stopped when he saw Emma.

"Sheila says you're doing a great job. Come out with us later today. We're going to shut down early and head over to the 110 Grill for Friday happy hour. Drinks are on me."

Emma smiled. "I'd love to, thank you."

"Great, we're heading over by four at the latest. Grab Sheila and we'll see you there."

Justin was all energy and enthusiasm. When he left the lobby to go back to his office, the room felt so quiet, like a balloon that lost all its air. Until Alyssa walked up and the phone rang.

"I've got it," Alyssa said.

Emma headed back to her desk and ate the sandwich that she'd brought with her. She dove back into her work and wanted to finish as much as possible before the day ended, especially if they were closing earlier than usual.

Sheila popped by a few minutes later.

"We're shutting down early today. Justin said he invited you to join us for drinks. He does this once a month or so. It should be a fun time. We can walk over together."

"Okay. I've actually never been to the 110."

Sheila smiled. "Oh, it's fun. Justin makes it fun. You'll see. He brings the party no matter where we go. And he insists on paying for everything. He's very generous."

She went back to her office and Emma went back to her typing. She finished up at a few minutes before four and began shutting down her computer. Sheila stopped by a minute later and Alyssa joined them and they walked over to the 110 together. The bar was big and they took up most of it. Justin told everyone to order whatever they wanted for drinks and he put in a few orders of appetizers for people to share, nachos, fries, wings.

Emma had a glass of La Crema chardonnay and Sheila and Alyssa both had cosmopolitans. Emma could handle just a sip of the sugary vodka drink. It was stronger than she liked for a whole drink, though. She tended to avoid vodka as it went right to her head. Wine was a slower buzz. She could sip a glass of wine slowly, and she wanted to be careful to pay close attention and not miss anything. But when Sheila finished her drink quickly and wondered aloud if she should have another or switch to wine, Emma encouraged her to have another.

"It looks really good. I'm not really a vodka drinker, but that is such a pretty drink."

Sheila laughed. "It tastes as good as it looks. Okay, I'll have another."

Justin walked over then and put his arm around Sheila. "Of course you will. We're just getting started. And you'll have another wine, too, right?" He met Emma's gaze and smiled, and she marveled at his charisma. When Justin looked her in the eye, it made her feel like she was the only person in the room. It was hard to say no to that. So she nodded. "Sure, that would be great, thanks!"

"Excellent!" Justin flagged the bartender, put their order in, and then wandered off to chat with someone else.

"He's so full of energy," Emma said.

Sheila laughed. "He is that. I tell him he's like a

Tasmanian devil sometimes, going in a million different directions. He's effective, though. Justin gets things done."

They chatted for a while, and Sheila's second martini went down almost as quickly as her first. She didn't even hesitate to order another this time.

"Three is my limit. I'll sleep well tonight. Peter has the kids, so I can indulge a little. And it's been a long week."

Alyssa saw a friend at the bar and excused herself to go say hello. That gave Emma an opportunity to ask about Mickey. She was curious what Sheila would say, if anything.

"What was that guy here for earlier? The older gentleman. He said he was a private detective."

Sheila looked sad for a moment and hesitated before saying, "I guess it doesn't hurt to tell you, as it's not anything confidential. He was here to help investigate Nancy's murder. Her mother hired his agency. And I did have some new information for him."

Emma was about to take a sip of wine, but set her glass down instead. "What new information?"

"Well, I'd already talked to the police with this update too. I was going through Nancy's emails yesterday afternoon looking for something for one of her clients. They said they'd emailed her a document a while back, and I found it, but I also saw something else. It was an email exchange with some guy she was seeing, evidently. They were making plans to meet for drinks and he said something about going to the same place they'd been to before, where they wouldn't run into anyone they knew. Makes me think maybe the guy was married or something."

"She never mentioned him to you?"

"No, and I thought she told me everything. But if this guy was married, well, she knows I don't like that. Peter cheated on me. That's one of the reasons we split, so she knew it was a sore spot. But yeah, she never mentioned him to me before. The name didn't ring any bells, Owen Sturgess."

Owen Sturgess. That Owen. Deadbeat husband of Claire Sturgess.

"How weird," Emma said.

"I know, right? So now the police have something new to look into. They haven't turned up anything yet, as far as I know."

"Hopefully, they'll find something soon," Emma said.

CHAPTER 14

Lee had invited Cindy and Emma to come to her appetizer party around seven on Saturday night. She said she'd invited a bigger crowd of people than usual, some other neighbors they only knew in passing, and she made a point of inviting Rich Gregory, the new neighbor and handsome Plymouth police detective.

It had taken Cindy longer than usual to decide what to wear. She finally settled on her most flattering soft faded jeans and a pretty flowered top in varying shades of blue, her favorite color.

Emma arrived just as Cindy was coming downstairs and heading toward the kitchen to take her artichoke and spinach dip out of the oven. Emma was carrying a dip too, a seven-layer taco dip that was good cold. She set it on the island along with a bag of tortilla chips and settled into one of the chairs and watched as her mother opened the oven.

"Artichoke and spinach—my favorite. Smells amazing. It looks done to me."

The casserole was golden and bubbling. Cindy grabbed two potholders and carefully took it out of the oven and set it on the stovetop to cool.

"You look really nice. I haven't seen you wear that top in ages," Emma said.

"Thanks, honey. It has been too long since I've worn this one. I always loved it."

Cindy found the glass lid for the casserole dish and carefully put it into a wicker basket for easy carrying to Lee's house.

Emma watched her silently and looked deep in thought for a few minutes. Finally she spoke, "So, I've been thinking about Owen. Did you let Claire know yet?"

"I did. I called her right after we spoke yesterday." Emma had called her on the way home from work and filled her in on what she'd learned from Sheila. "She doesn't think Owen had anything to do with Nancy's murder, but it wouldn't surprise her one bit if he dated her. She said he admitted to using a dating site when he first asked for a divorce, but now he says he'd deny it and she'd never be able to prove it. He's been quite a jerk evidently."

"But even if he had nothing to do with the murder, it might help Claire's case if he admits to dating Nancy? Or maybe to clear his name, he'll spill the details and admit that he's dating someone else?" Emma wondered aloud.

"Or he could lie and refuse to admit anything," Cindy

said. "And I'll be shocked if he agrees to talk to Mickey. Though, of course, I hope he does."

"I wonder what he will say to the police?"

"I imagine we'll find out soon enough." Cindy picked up the basket. "Are you ready to go?"

A few minutes later they arrived at Lee's house. It was only ten minutes past seven, but there were already a dozen or so people there.

"You can set everything on the kitchen table or island wherever you can find a free spot. Help yourselves to whatever you want to drink." Lee said before going to answer a knock at the front door.

Cindy and Emma set their dips and chips down and helped themselves to some chardonnay. They sipped their wine and looked around the room. The first familiar face they saw was Rachel's, and she came over as soon as she saw them.

"Rich is here. That police detective. We were just chatting a bit. He seems like a nice guy. You should talk to him. I don't think he knows all that many people here, other than Bob."

Cindy hadn't seen Rich yet, but as Rachel was talking, she saw him pass by on his way to the food table.

"Let's go get some food and find a place to sit and chat," Emma suggested. "I don't know about you two, but I'm starving."

"I am too. I haven't tried anything yet," Rachel agreed.

Cindy followed them into the kitchen and they all grabbed paper plates and filled them with food. There were so many appetizers and dips to choose from. Whenever Lee had her parties, she encouraged everyone to bring their favorite appetizers, which made for a good variety.

Cindy had a full plate and was debating between adding a few cocktail shrimp or steak on a stick when an amused voice behind her said, "I just had the shrimp and steak, I'd get them both."

She turned and Rich was standing there, holding a beer in one hand, a paper plate with a slice of pizza in the other.

"Good to know, thanks. It's Rich right?" she asked.

He nodded. "Yes and it's Cindy?"

"Yes."

"Why don't you come sit with us?" Emma suggested. She led them to an outside table on Lee's back patio. Rachel excused herself just as they were sitting, to go say hello to someone. Once they were settled, they all chatted for a few minutes about nothing in particular. And then Emma asked him about Owen.

"Have you talked to him yet?"

Rich looked surprised by the question. "How do you know about Owen Sturgess?"

Emma smiled, somewhat smugly, Cindy thought. "We have our ways."

"Right. Okay. Yes, we talked to him late yesterday afternoon, actually." He took a sip of his beer and looked like he wanted to change the subject, but Emma wouldn't allow it.

"What did he say? Did he admit to dating Nancy?" she asked eagerly.

Rich sighed. "He didn't admit to much. He did say he and Nancy went out a few times. Says he was at home the night Nancy disappeared. But his wife said he wasn't with her."

"Can anyone corroborate his story?" Emma asked.

"He gave us a name. A young woman, Amber Thomas. We're talking to her on Monday."

"Do you think he's involved?" Emma asked.

Rich shook his head. "Probably not, but I've been surprised before. So, we talk to everyone, consider everything."

"We were already following Owen." Emma told him about their surveillance case for Claire.

That seemed to intrigue Rich. "Have you talked to him?"

"No, we weren't planning on it before, but now of course we'd like to. It could help both cases if he agrees to talk to us."

Rich nodded. "It could, but I wouldn't hold your breath on that. If he does though, please let us know if you learn anything useful."

Before Emma could speak, Cindy jumped in. "Of course we will," she said with a smile.

Emma stood and excused herself. "I'm going for more wine. Do either of you need anything?" Rich still had a full beer and Cindy had barely touched hers.

"Okay, I'll be back in a bit," Emma left and then it was just the two of them. They'd both finished eating and were sipping their drinks. Rich didn't seem in any hurry to get up and mingle.

"So, tell me more about yourself. I didn't realize when I stopped by your office the other day that we were practically neighbors. Have you lived in the Pinehills long?" he asked her.

"A little over thirty years. I love it here."

"Do you golf?"

She laughed. "Sort of, but not really. We're just taking golf lessons now. Me, Lee and Rachel. We've lived here for so long and are only just now getting around to it."

Rich smiled. "It's a great game. You all might want to join a ladies league. There's one or two here, and you don't have to be an expert. That's what handicaps are for."

"So, I hear. Maybe next year. We still need to get on the course and play an actual round of golf first."

He laughed. "Well, that would help."

A few minutes later, Rachel, Lee and Bob joined them and as a group, they laughed and chatted for the next few hours. Emma left after an hour or so to go meet up with her brother and Dana downtown, and Cindy couldn't remember the last time she'd had so much fun. Rich was easy to talk to and funny. When the party wound down and people started leaving, he asked to walk her home.

"My car is at the end of the street, so I think I'm probably walking by your house anyway," he said.

A few minutes later, they reached her front door.

"I almost didn't come to this tonight. I'm not usually

good with parties, and I really only knew Bob. But, I'm glad that I did. I really enjoyed talking with you."

Cindy felt herself blush a little and was glad it was too dark out for him to see it.

"I did too. We were saying the other day that we've lived here for so long and don't know as many people as we should. So, I'm glad you came too."

Rich was quiet for a moment, and it was too dark for her to see his expression well.

"I'm very rusty at this. But would you like to go out to dinner sometime?"

Cindy was happily surprised by the invitation.

"I'm rusty too. And yes, I'd love to go to dinner with you."

He grinned. "Great, I'll call you next week. We'll make a plan."

"Sounds good."

He waited for her to step inside and as she locked the front door, she watched through the window as he turned to walk to his car. And then she smiled. She had a date. First one in a very long time.

"You're going out with Rich?" Emma was surprised and intrigued. Her mother had just finished telling her about the rest of the evening at Lee's and the dinner invitation. Emma refilled her coffee mug and settled back on the soft leather sofa. They were in the office Monday morning and Mickey hadn't arrived yet.

Her mother looked like she was having second thoughts, though.

"Are you sure it's a good idea? I've been thinking about it all weekend and I'm not sure it is. I mean, isn't it a conflict of interest, maybe?"

Emma grinned. "No. You just have cold feet. If anything, it's a good thing. You'll get to date a guy that seems nice and isn't bad looking at all, and we might get the inside track on what's really going on with some of our investigations."

Her mother looked worried about that though, too. "That doesn't seem right. I don't want to expect any special favors."

"And I'm sure you won't get any. Rich has been with the force for years. He's not going to share anything that he shouldn't. It will be good to have someone on the inside."

"I just want to have a nice dinner and conversation. Let's not get ahead of ourselves."

Mickey arrived a few minutes later and Emma filled him in on her day at the law firm on Friday and what they learned from Rich at the party.

"So, we'll try to talk to Owen today then. I'll call him now. And Amber too."

They watched as Mickey dialed Owen's number. He answered quickly.

"Owen Sturgess? Mickey McConnell here from Court Street Investigations. I'd like to meet with you ideally today or tomorrow. It shouldn't take too much of your time. It's about the Nancy Eldridge investigation." Mickey was quiet for a minute before saying, "Yes, I know you already talked to the police. We are actually retained by Nancy's mother. She's anxious to get this solved as soon as possible." Mickey frowned as Owen talked, and Emma wished she could hear both sides of the conversation.

"Okay, well if you change your mind, please let me know." He ended the call and wasn't happy. "Owen says he doesn't have to talk to us and already talked to the police."

"Oh, that's too bad," Emma said.

"I'll call Claire and let her know. Maybe she can convince him to talk to us," her mother said. She went off and made the call and was back a few minutes later. "She said she'll talk to him, but told us not to get our hopes up. He's been especially difficult lately." They'd given Claire all the evidence they'd collected on Owen and Amber, and she handed it to her lawyer. It was still going to be an expensive divorce for Claire, but the more she could show about Owen that could help her case, the better.

They had a new skip-tracing case to work on, so Emma and Mickey both got busy online and the morning flew. By early afternoon, they had the new case almost wrapped up and Mickey was getting ready to leave for the day when his cell phone rang and he winked at Emma as he saw the caller ID and answered the phone.

"Owen, good to hear from you."

CHAPTER 15

The next morning at a few minutes before ten, Mickey and Emma pulled up to Owen's house. There was only one car in the driveway, an older model silver Mercedes convertible. Mickey was driving his convertible too, as they didn't want to risk Owen recognizing Emma's car.

Mickey parked next to Owen's car, and they made their way to the front door. Emma rang the doorbell. There was no response for several minutes and Emma was about to ring the bell again when the door opened and Owen stood there, in bare feet, sweatpants and a blue Boston College sweatshirt. He looked freshly showered as his graying black hair was still damp and combed back.

"Come on in. We can sit in the kitchen. Coffee? I just made some."

Emma and Mickey both declined.

They sat at the small round wooden table in Owen's

kitchen. Mickey got out his well-worn black leather note-book and opened it to a blank page. He fished a silver engraved Cross pen out of his pocket and set it on the page. Emma pulled out her smart phone and set it on the table.

"Do you mind if we record this?" she asked.

Owen seemed surprised by the question and hesitated a moment. Finally, he shrugged. "Sure, why not?"

Emma clicked on record as Mickey began the meeting.

"First of all, thank you for meeting with us. I know you've already talked to the police. Nancy's mother is devastated, as you can imagine. So we are going over everything with a fine-tooth comb to see what we might have missed."

Owen nodded and took a sip of his coffee.

Mickey began with the questions. "So, you knew Nancy?"

"I did."

"What was the nature of your relationship?"

"We met on a dating site. For busy professionals. Nancy worked long hours, so it was hard for her to meet someone. And I wasn't looking for anything serious."

Mickey raised his eyebrows. "Are you still married?"

"Yes, but we are going through a divorce."

"I see. And Nancy knew this?"

"Yes. We were discreet. We only went out a few times."

"Why did things end?"

"She met my wife. Claire was referred to her for the divorce."

"She was Claire's divorce attorney?" Emma said. That added a new wrinkle.

He nodded. "Yeah. Nancy said it was too much of a conflict for her to continue seeing me as Claire was her client. I understood."

"Who is her attorney now?" Mickey asked.

"Someone else in the firm stepped in when Nancy died. I think it was one of the owners, Justin something."

Mickey took a moment to jot that down in his notebook. Emma preferred to use a recorder, so there would be nothing lost in translation.

"Where were you the night of Nancy's murder?" Mickey asked.

Owen smiled. "I was here, with Amber."

"And who is Amber?"

"That's who I'm currently dating. We met on the same site. She lives out of state but comes to see me when she can, usually on weekends."

"Nancy died on a Wednesday night," Mickey said.

"That was a week that Amber was here. Sometimes if she doesn't have any client visits scheduled, she spends most of the week here. She has the flexibility to work from home."

"So, she was here then. Did anyone else see you at home that night?"

Owen thought for a moment. "No, not that I recall."

Mickey glanced at Emma before saying, "So, you only have Amber's word to back this up?"

"I didn't kill Nancy!" Owen snapped. He ran a hand through his hair and took a breath. "Look, I had nothing to do with it. I hadn't seen Nancy in months. And I liked her. I don't have a motive."

"What did you think of Nancy's work on the divorce?" Emma asked.

Owen laughed bitterly. "She was a very good lawyer."

"How long have you been dating Amber?" Mickey asked.

Owen thought about it for a moment. "About two months."

"And you said she lives here when she comes to visit? Spends the week or weekend? Things are serious with you two?" Emma asked.

"That's right," Owen confirmed.

Emma glanced at Mickey. He nodded, and she picked up her phone, but it was still recording.

"I think we are all set. Unless there's anything else you can think of that might be helpful?" Emma asked.

"I've told you everything. Like I said, I have nothing to hide."

Mickey stood and held out his hand. Owen shook it. "Thank you for meeting with us. If you do think of anything else—anything at all—please give me a call. He handed Owen one of his business cards and they left.

Once they were in Mickey's car, driving back to the office, Emma asked what he thought about Owen.

"Well, he's not someone I'd want a granddaughter of mine to date, but I doubt he had anything to do with killing Nancy."

"He sort of has a motive, though. If she was doing too good of a job for Claire with the divorce. She said he was counting on getting a big settlement and alimony."

"Hmm. It's possible. But I still don't think he's our guy. We won't rule him out entirely, though. Especially as the only person that can confirm his alibi is his girlfriend."

Emma brightened up at the mention of Amber. "So, I got it on tape that she's practically living with him and he gave us permission to record."

Mickey smiled. "He did, didn't he? Hopefully it will be useful information for her lawyer. If it reduces Owen's settlement, well, I won't feel bad about that at all."

It had been a very long time since Cindy felt anything remotely like butterflies in her stomach. But as she was getting ready to go on her first date with Rich Gregory, she felt them and it surprised her. She was a little nervous but also excited too, and she wanted to look nice. She tried on several sweaters before settling on a pretty light green cashmere one, and she paired it with charcoal gray pants. She curled her hair just a little, to give it some body, and she was applying her favorite rosy pink lipstick when she heard a knock on the front door. Rich had arrived. She gave her hair a final brushing and headed downstairs to open the door.

He looked nice. He was wearing a navy blazer and a light yellow button-down shirt and tan pants. And he smelled good. She couldn't place the cologne, but it smelled freshly applied, and that made her smile.

"You look great," he said appreciatively.

"Thank you. You're looking handsome too."

Rich looked around her downstairs. It was an open floor plan, and the kitchen opened into the living room. He smiled,

"I have almost the same layout, but in reverse." Many of the units at the Pinehills had similar layouts and were built by the same developer.

"You have good taste," she teased him.

He laughed. "I like to think so. Are you ready to go?"

"I'm ready. I'll just grab my purse and we can go."

Rich drove and she climbed into his Audi sedan and they headed to downtown Plymouth.

"Have you been to the Cork and Table yet? I thought that might be a good spot for us to go. The food is really good, and it's small, so the service is great too."

"Yes, I've been there a few times. I love it."

Rich had made a reservation and when they arrived, they were seated right away at one of the few window seats, which overlooked Main Street, so they could see people walking by.

Rich ordered a beer and Cindy got a glass of chardonnay. When their server brought the drinks, she told them the specials of the day and gave them a few more minutes to decide.

"Do you want to share an appetizer?" Rich asked. "I was looking at the pimento cheese. I haven't had that before, have you?"

Cindy nodded. "Yes, and it's delicious. This place is owned by a husband and wife that moved here from the Charleston area. So some of their dishes reflect that, like the pimento cheese."

"Great, let's get that then. Do you know what you want for your main course?"

"Yes. I always get the same thing here—the shrimp and grits. I went to Charleston a few years ago and had it everywhere. What about you?"

"She mentioned a veal shank special. That sounded good to me."

When the waitress returned, they put in their order and a few minutes later, she brought their appetizer out, warmed pimento cheese with crusty bread for spreading.

"How did you decide to be a police officer?" Cindy asked as she spread some savory cheese on her bread.

"My father was a Boston cop. I always admired him and his pride in his job. I knew from a young age that I wanted to do it too. My parents insisted that I go to college, and I did, but it never changed my mind."

"They must have been proud of you. Your father especially."

"He never saw it. My father died unexpectedly when I was a senior in college. It was on the job. He responded to a domestic violence call and was helping a mother and her two kids get out of the house when her crazy husband pulled out a gun and shot him. He was killed instantly."

"Oh no! I'm so sorry. That must have been so hard. I can't imagine."

He nodded. "It was awful. My mother tried to talk me

out of going into the police academy after that. But I was even more committed to it. My father saved lives. What he did mattered."

Cindy smiled. "As a mother, I probably would have tried to talk you out of it, too."

"Domestic violence calls are probably the most dangerous ones we go on. When someone is in that kind of state, they're not thinking. They're just reacting. We never respond alone. That's one thing that has changed. My dad was by himself. Another officer was on the way. We go in as a team and have each other's back."

"That sounds smart. Tell me about your family? Do you have any children?"

"I do. Two girls, Anne and Hannah. They don't live too far away. One's in Duxbury and the other is in Scituate. They're both married, no kids yet though."

Cindy knew he was divorced, but didn't feel comfortable asking him about it.

"I have the two, Emma and Matt. Neither one is married, but I think Matt is getting close. He's pretty serious with his girlfriend Dana. Emma just recently moved home from L.A. and I don't think she's dating anyone yet. Fred and I divorced many years ago. He was a great guy, but it just didn't work with us."

"You must have had a pretty good relationship if he left the business to you both?"

"We always got along well enough. I used to help him with the business a little when we were married, and I think he liked the idea of Emma and I working together. It was very generous of him."

Rich smiled. "And Emma moved home to be a PI?"

"She did. She gave it a real shot in Hollywood, though. She'd always dreamed of being an actress. And she worked a little here and there, commercials, bit parts. But it never really happened for her. It doesn't for most people. And she used to love working with her father. So, I think maybe things work out the way they are supposed to."

"I think they probably do. Did you have a different career before this?"

"I have a yoga studio in the Pinehills. I started it when I was married as a part-time thing, and then it turned into a real business. I still have that going as well."

"You're a busy lady. And yoga. That explains why you're in such good shape. My ex-wife was into yoga. We divorced when the kids went to college. We probably should have done it years before that. Courtney hated my job. She always tried to get me to quit and do something else. We were college sweethearts and probably got married much too young. But then the girls came right away, and we were just busy with them."

"Have you dated much, since then?" Cindy asked tentatively. She realized she didn't know much about Rich. Maybe he went on dates all the time. She thought of Owen and the online site that Emma said he used to meet women. Rachel had done that a bit, but Cindy was too nervous to try it.

Rich laughed. "No, not much. Here and there I've gone out to dinner or a movie, but there was never that spark that you want. What about you?"

"Same. I really haven't dated much at all. When I was first divorced I did a bit, but wasn't ready. Then when I did feel ready, I lost my nerve to put myself out there. A friend of mine is dating up a storm, though. She uses one of those online sites. She keeps trying to get me to do it too."

"Well, selfishly, I hope you won't. I don't want any competition."

Cindy smiled and said nothing. But she felt a warm glow. She thought the date was going pretty well, and that seemed like a good sign that there could be a second date.

Their plates were empty and when the server came and cleared them, she asked if they wanted dessert.

"I think I'm too full," Cindy said. She'd eaten every drop of her shrimp and grits.

"I'm pretty full too, but I have a hard time not getting crème brûlée when it's on the menu. I'll have one, but bring two spoons. Maybe I can tempt her." Their waitress went off to put their order in and returned a few minutes later with the dessert. Crème brûlée was one of Cindy's favorites too, so she didn't hesitate to pick up a spoon and take a taste.

When they finished, Rich insisted on paying the bill, even though Cindy offered.

"Thank you. It was wonderful."

They headed home and Rich walked her to her door.

"Thank you for coming out with me tonight. If you're up for it, I'd love to do it again sometime?"

Cindy felt the warm glow again. "Yes, I'd love to go out again. This was really fun."

Rich leaned over and kissed her lightly on the cheek.

"Goodnight, Cindy. I'll give you a call soon."

She was about to step inside when Rich turned back.

"I meant to ask you earlier. What did Mickey and Emma think of Owen Sturgess? Have they talked to him yet?"

"They did. They both think he's kind of a jerk, but weren't convinced that he has anything to do with Nancy's death. Though we were all surprised to find out that Nancy was Claire Sturgess's divorce lawyer. She'd hired us to find out how serious things are with his new girlfriend. If they might be living together. The divorce sounds pretty ugly."

Rich nodded. "We already talked to him and he wasn't at the top of our list. But we've just moved him up a notch. A bartender at East Bay Grille stopped in to confidentially share a conversation she overheard. Owen was talking to a friend at the bar about his divorce and he was really upset. And he mentioned Nancy's name. Said he didn't think she'd go after him so hard."

"That doesn't sound too bad. He was probably just venting, upset about the divorce not going his way."

"Right. But then he said, I feel like killing her right now. I really do."

"What? Who did he mean? Nancy or Claire?" Cindy asked.

"His friend at the bar asked the same thing. He said both of them. And the bartender said he had a look in his eyes that made her nervous."

Cindy shivered as she felt a sudden chill in the air.

"Well, that's not good."

CHAPTER 16

"So, tell me all about it? Where did you go? What did you have? And what did you think about him?" Emma fired off the questions as soon as her mother was seated and about to take her first sip of coffee. It was Saturday morning, and they were on the deck of Emma's cottage. It was an absolutely gorgeous morning, warmer than usual, so when she called her mother to see how the date went, Emma suggested she come over for coffee instead and they could chat in person and enjoy the morning.

The beach was already busy with people walking, dogs running in and out of the surf and children playing. Oscar was sound asleep in a sunny spot on the deck and barely twitched his tail when her mother arrived.

"It was really nice. Better than I'd expected. I think we were both a little nervous." She told Emma all about the date and had her dying to go there soon for the shrimp and grits and pimento cheese.

"I'm glad you had a good time. Do you think you'll see him again? Do you want to?"

Her mother smiled. "He mentioned going out again, and yes, I would like a second date. He's easy company."

Emma laughed. "He's easy on the eyes, too, Mom."

Her mother looked a little embarrassed. "Yes, he is, isn't he?" She glanced at Oscar and changed the subject. "Did you get a cat?"

"That's Oscar. We've sort of adopted each other. He started coming every morning for breakfast and last night, when it started raining, he came to the door and I let him in. So, I think he might be mine now."

"His coloring is very pretty, sort of creamy orange."

Emma steered the conversation back to Rich. "Did Rich mention any updates on Nancy's case?"

"He did, actually. A bartender from East Bay overheard a conversation at the bar between Owen and a friend." When her mother finished sharing what the bartender overheard, Emma felt herself shiver. And it wasn't just because clouds suddenly rolled in and blocked the sun. She could picture Owen's expression, and she wondered what he was capable of.

"Did Rich think there was anything to it?"

"He didn't say. He was just surprised to hear it and said it has moved him up a little on their list."

"Who is at the top?"

"I think it's still Peter, Sheila's husband. Rich didn't say anything about that though."

"We'll have to sit down with Mickey first thing

Monday morning and strategize where to go next on this. I feel like we still have a lot of digging to do," Emma said.

"Good morning, ladies!" Emma turned at the sound of the familiar voice. Brady stepped onto his deck and waved at Emma and her mom. He was wearing sweats and a t-shirt and looked like he'd just come home from the gym.

"Is that Brady?" Her mother whispered.

Emma nodded. "Brady, come meet my mom."

"I'll be right over."

Less than two minutes later, he stepped onto Emma's deck and flashed his slow, charming smile her mother's way as Emma made the introductions and they shook hands.

"Do you want some coffee?" Emma offered.

Brady shook his head. "No, I had a few cups already, before I hit the gym. I'll stay and chat for a minute though." He slid into the empty seat next to Emma.

"I'm glad Emma has someone she knows for a neighbor," her mother said. "I was a little worried when she first told me she'd rented one of these cottages, as most of them are only occupied in the summer."

Brady grinned. "I was glad when she moved in too. It does get a little quiet down here in the off-season. I don't mind it though."

"A few more weeks and it will be busy all the time," her mother said. "Have you lived here yet for the third of July?"

Brady laughed. "Yes, and it's as crazy as ever. It's nice

to be right here, yet able to go inside when you've had enough of it."

"It's been years since I've been here on the third," Emma said. "I'm looking forward to it." She glanced at her mother. "I'll definitely have a cookout and have everyone over. Plan on spending the day at the beach and the night watching the fireworks."

"Will you have people over then, too?" Emma's mother asked Brady.

He nodded. "Everyone I know comes over then, including my mother. She looks forward to it."

They chatted a bit longer and then Brady's watch beeped. "That's my mother calling. I'm heading over there shortly to help her with a gardening project. So, I should be on my way." He stood to go and looked back at Emma.

"If you're not doing anything later, I was thinking of taking a drive down to Fisherman's View in Sandwich. Have you been there? It's on the canal and a buddy told me I have to try their lobster sushi roll. Any interest in joining me?"

Emma had no plans and welcomed the chance to do something.

"I haven't been there yet. Would love to go."

"Great, I'll check in with you later." He glanced at Emma's mother. "It was nice meeting you."

Once he left, Emma's mother raised her eyebrows. "Is there something you need to tell me?"

Emma laughed. "What? No. There's nothing with me

and Brady. We're just friends and neighbors, and I'm just glad to have something to do tonight."

"Well, he seems charming enough. Handsome, too. Isn't he the one though that your brother warned you to stay away from?"

"Yes, he's the one. I don't think Matt really knows Brady though."

"Maybe not, but be careful, honey. If you are interested in him as more than friends, go slowly. It's been many years since you and Brady were in school together. You don't really know him all that well, either."

Her mother had a good point.

Emma smiled. "It's just dinner. That lobster sushi roll sounds good."

BRADY STOPPED BY ON HIS WAY HOME FROM HIS MOTHER'S later that afternoon and they agreed to head to the Fisherman's View around six. Emma knew this wasn't a date, just two neighbors getting a bite to eat, but she still found herself taking more time than usual trying to decide what to wear. She finally settled on an old pair of jeans that were soft and flattering and a pink cashmere v-neck sweater.

Oscar showed up at the back door and she fed him and made sure he was inside before she left. Brady knocked on her door at six sharp and they headed out. He drove and chatted most of the way during the twenty or so minute drive. They turned left on route 3A and meandered along until they reached Cedarville and jumped on the highway for the last ten minutes or so, over the Cape Cod Canal and on to Sandwich.

Fisherman's View was located on the canal and there was a great view of the boats going by. The restaurant was busy but two seats opened up at the long bar and they decided to eat there. Otherwise, the wait was at least an hour for a table.

A bartender came right over once they were seated and Emma ordered a chardonnay and Brady got a local draft beer. Even though they were inside at the bar, they still had good water views. And the menu was extensive, with all kinds of seafood and lobster dishes. They decided to stay with appetizers and sushi and ordered the cooked lobster sushi roll and a spicy tuna roll, shrimp cocktail and an order of crab cakes.

"So where did you go this week?" Emma asked. She'd noticed that Brady had been out of town for a few days.

"Kansas City to a medical software client. They are doing a go-live for a new customer and needed something to integrate better."

Emma laughed. "That all sounds like Greek to me. But it went well?"

He nodded. "It was a little hairy at first. But I was able to get it sorted out for them."

The bartender set down their shrimp cocktail a moment later, and they dug in. The shrimp were huge. Emma glanced out the window and saw a tugboat pulling a big barge. They could see the barges go by from their cottages too, but far off in the distance. Here they were so close they could see the names on the various shipping containers.

"So, how are you liking being back in Plymouth? Do you think you might stay?" Brady asked.

Emma nodded. "I do. Now that I'm back, it almost feels like I never left, but in a good way. I don't think I could go back to living in California again."

"You don't miss the whole Hollywood life?"

She laughed at the thought. "I don't, at all. I do miss the work a little. But I don't miss the lifestyle. I'm very happy to be home. And I'm having fun at the agency. I like working with Mickey and my mom."

"How old is Mickey? He's a character."

"Just about eighty. He's awesome. He's been a good teacher. He's still sharp as a tack."

They both looked up as the bartender set down a platter between them with their sushi rolls. Emma had never had a lobster sushi roll before and it was so good, with big chunks of sweet lobster in the middle and a sliver of fresh tuna across the top.

They both agreed the sushi was amazing and Emma was already starting to feel full by the time the bartender brought out the crab cakes. Those were also delicious, but she was glad they were splitting them.

When their plates were empty and their drinks almost gone too, the bartender returned and asked if they wanted anything else.

"What do you think? Do you feel like another drink?" Brady asked. "We could sit and relax for a bit before heading home."

"Sure." It was still early. The sun was just going down and Emma wasn't ready to go home yet.

"Did you stay in Plymouth after graduation? Or move back here recently?" Emma asked. She was curious to know more about Brady and what he'd been up to since they went to school together.

"No, I moved to Boston right after graduation and took a job with Accenture on their technology team. Lived right downtown in the Back Bay and worked out of the Prudential Center."

"I bet it was fun living in Boston. Did you love it?"

He smiled. "I did. It was a great place to work and for a kid right out of school it was fun being in the city. I traveled even more then. We were road warriors, flying out most weeks on Sunday night and back home on Fridays. And then we ran around Boston all weekend."

Emma could picture Brady taking Boston by storm with his friends. She thought it sounded fun, except for all that travel.

"So, you've always traveled then. You don't mind it?" she asked.

"I didn't mind it then. It was exciting going to so many new places and different companies. But a few years ago I got sick of living in the city. My mother had a health scare, and I wanted to be closer."

"Oh, I didn't know that. She's okay now?"

"Yeah, she's fine now. The good thing about what I do is that I can live anywhere really and either deal with clients remotely or jump on a plane. I work for myself now and have a handful of key clients, and don't have to travel like I used to. So it's all good."

"Do you have any brothers or sisters?" Emma didn't think that he did, but wasn't sure.

"No, it's just me. And my mom. I lost my father too, but I was so young that I barely remember him."

"I'm sorry. I didn't know that. It seems like you and your mom are pretty close. You see her often?"

He smiled at the mention of his mother. "I do. She's incredible. We talk every day or so and I see her at least once a week, usually more. I drop by sometimes over the weekend and she loves that. She loves to go out to eat, so we have a few favorite places in the rotation."

Brady's face softened when he talked about his mother. It was clear that he adored her and that made Emma like him even more. She was close to her mother too. She'd been close to her father as well, but not like her mother.

"What are her favorite places?"

"That's easy. She loves 42 Degrees North, and Cafe Strega. Or if we want to be down on the waterfront, either the Blue-Eyed Crab or East Bay."

"All good choices."

"If I'm around, anytime you feel like grabbing a bite, just holler. I'm always up for going out," Brady said. His easy smile lit up his face and Emma felt a twinge of something, butterflies maybe? She forced the feeling down, though. Brady was her neighbor. A good friend to hang out with, and share a meal or a drink now and then. And she welcomed that.

"Good to know. I'll remember that."

The conversation turned to people they both knew from high school and where they were now. Brady had kept in touch with quite a few people and kept Emma laughing with his stories. Before she knew it, the sun had set, and their glasses were empty. It was time to go home.

The ride home was comfortable. They chatted easily and soon they were on Taylor Avenue, parking and walking to their cottages. Brady walked Emma to her door and waited until she was inside.

"I'm glad we did this, Emma. It was a fun night. Remember, anytime you want to do it again, let me know."

"It was fun, and I will. Goodnight, Brady." Emma closed the door behind her and watched out the window as Brady walked to his cottage and disappeared inside. Something soft brushed against her leg and she jumped. She looked down to see Oscar staring up at her, demanding to be petted.

"You startled me. Let's go settle down, Oscar." Emma went into her bedroom, changed into comfy pajamas then curled up on the living room sofa to watch TV for a bit before bed. Oscar hopped up next to her. She reached for the remote and started clicking through channels to find something that looked good. Finally, she found a movie on Netflix and as it started, she saw movement outside and realized Brady had just walked out onto his deck. He was only out there for a few minutes before heading back inside.

She'd really enjoyed Brady's company. More than

she'd expected. And she liked that he was so close to his mother. She was glad that he was living next door and a new friend for her to do things with. She thought about her own mother and her reminder that Matt wasn't a fan of Brady at all. Emma dismissed the thought. Her brother clearly didn't have all the information. The Brady she was getting to know seemed like such a good guy.

CHAPTER 17

Emma stopped at Clements, the neighborhood grocery store, on the way to the office. She picked up a healthy selection of snacks—carrot and celery sticks, some veggie sushi and air-popped popcorn. But then she walked by the bakery and they were just putting out freshly-baked muffins and she couldn't resist. She picked up pistachio nut muffins for everyone in the office.

Her mother was already in the office, and raised her eyebrow when she saw Emma set the box of muffins on the coffee table.

"I got healthy stuff too. But these are still warm, and it's a Monday. We deserve a treat."

Mickey didn't hesitate to reach for a muffin. "I quite agree. Thank you, Emma."

Her mother laughed. "Fine. I'll have one too."

Emma made herself a coffee and joined the others in the middle of the room where they were already seated on the sofa and chair. They'd gotten into the habit of holding Monday morning meetings to go over status updates and look at the week ahead.

Just as they were about to start the meeting, the office line rang. Emma's mother answered the call and after a moment, it was easy to tell that it was Belinda Russell.

"Okay, thank you for that update. We will keep digging to see what we can find out."

"Did Belinda get an update from the police?" Emma asked when her mother sat back down.

"She did. She said the police don't know if there's a connection, but they are looking more closely now at Justin Powell, Nancy's boss. It seems that he has some kind of Ponzi scheme going possibly with some of his company's clients.

It came to their attention because one of his clients, an Andrew Sinclair, had a friend in the FBI and mentioned that something didn't seem right about what Justin was doing. It was presented to him as an excellent investment opportunity, but he's thinking now that it's something else entirely. They've been slowly investigating and building a case."

"Does Belinda think that Nancy might have been involved? Maybe that's what got her killed?" Emma asked.

"She said that the police asked for her opinion on that and she doesn't think Nancy would have been involved in anything illegal."

"Maybe she found out and was going to blow the whistle?" Mickey said.

"That would give Justin motive. And he paid for the funeral, too. Maybe that was him feeling guilty," Emma said.

Her mother nodded. "It's possible. But Belinda thought the world of Justin and said he was always wonderful to Nancy. She could see him being involved in something shady because most lawyers don't make the kind of money Justin makes. But she doesn't think he could have hurt Nancy."

"You never know what people are capable of," Mickey said.

"I could call Rachel and see if she can get me back over there as a temp. She said they really liked me and they could definitely use me again if I was available."

"That's not a bad idea. You could snoop around a bit and see what you can uncover," Mickey said.

But her mother didn't look convinced. "I'm not sure that's a great idea, honey. If this guy Justin is involved with Nancy's death, I don't like the idea of you being around him. Especially if he finds out who you really are."

"Mom, he won't find out. I'll be very careful."

"Okay, but you don't have to do that. I really am not keen on the idea."

"Seriously, there is nothing to worry about. I'll probably just end up typing all day." Emma grinned. "That's about as safe as it gets."

"I think it's a great idea," Mickey said.

"All right. I'll give Rachel a call."

Two days later, Emma started a three-day assignment at the law firm. She'd be there Thursday, Friday and Monday.

Since Sheila supported Justin, as well as acted as office manager, Emma hoped she'd have a chance to snoop around Sheila's office-maybe at lunch if she went out.

But on Thursday and Friday, Sheila ate at her desk, so all Emma was able to do was sit and type all day.

But everyone was going to the 110 after work on Friday, so Emma happily accepted Sheila's invite to walk over with her.

Justin was already at the bar when they arrived and had ordered a bunch of food and a round of drinks for everyone.

They found two seats at the bar and put their drinks order in. Emma went with chardonnay like usual. Sheila got a cosmopolitan again.

The seat on the other side of Emma opened up and a moment later, Justin settled into it. He was drinking a martini on the rocks with extra olives.

"You came back! Sheila says you do great work. We're not looking for anyone full-time right now, but if you are interested, let Sheila know and she'll be in touch if something opens up."

Emma smiled and pretended to be grateful for the opportunity. "Thank you, I will do that."

"So, it's Emily, right?"

"Emma actually."

"Of course. So, Emma, what do you do for fun when you're not working?"

"Nothing too unusual. I live on the beach, so I like spending time there. And I go the gym sometimes and of course out to dinner."

"Do you like boats?"

"Sure."

"I just got a new yacht. Docked at the Plymouth marina. Biggest one I've had yet. It's a seventy-five footer. You ever been on a boat that big?"

"No, I can't say that I have. It sounds lovely." Emma couldn't begin to imagine how expensive a yacht that size must be. Several million, probably.

"It's insane. I'll be having a party on it soon. You should come."

Emma hesitated, not sure how to respond to that. But fortunately no response was necessary as someone tapped Justin on the shoulder and he was up and on his way to the other side of the bar.

"He's something, isn't he?" Sheila said with a look of amusement.

"He's very energetic," Emma said. She wasn't sure what was safe to say to Sheila. As she wasn't sure how close she and Justin were.

"I think he has ADHD, seriously. The man can't sit still for more than a few minutes at a time."

"He was telling me about his new boat. It sounds nice."

"It's extravagant. Over the top, like Justin. He had most of the office over last Friday night to celebrate the boat's christening. He has a driver for it and had a caterer to serve food and bartenders to keep the drinks flowing. We rode all around Plymouth Harbor for a few hours. It was fun."

"That does sound fun," Emma agreed. She noticed Justin high-fiving two of the junior lawyers after they all did shots.

"That's Justin. Life of the party. He was pouring shots on the boat too. The guys, especially the younger ones that work for him, love it."

"You're not fond of shots?" Emma asked with a smile.

Sheila laughed. "Hardly. It's been many years since I've done a shot. I'm too old for that. Or I should say, too mature. Justin is actually ten years older than me. You'd never know it by the way he acts, though. He's like a big kid sometimes."

"He is very enthusiastic," Emma agreed.

"He is. That's why I love working for him. He's very appreciative and there's never a dull moment."

"Have you heard anything about the investigation for Nancy? I wonder if the police are getting any closer," Emma said.

Sheila was quiet for a moment, then sighed heavily. "It doesn't sound like they are any closer. Last I heard they were talking to my ex-husband, which is ridiculous. He wasn't a fan of Nancy's but I'm sure Peter had nothing to do with it."

"He didn't like Nancy?"

"Not particularly. She was my divorce attorney, and she was very good." Sheila smiled and Emma sensed that

Sheila had made out better in the divorce than Peter did, thanks to Nancy.

"I think his dislike though was more that for a long time he was jealous of Nancy. When we separated, he didn't expect things to go so easily for me. We share custody and it was hard at first to get used to being a single mother."

"That must have been hard," Emma sympathized.

"It was. But Nancy was a godsend. I think he resented that she was always here, always helping if I needed someone to watch the kids last minute. Stuff like that. We were super tight and I think maybe he felt like I replaced him with Nancy. That I didn't need him."

"I'm guessing he didn't want the divorce?" Emma asked.

"No. I think he thought if it wasn't for Nancy, maybe we would have gotten back together. He said that once. But that's crazy. Nancy was just a great friend, always there for me. She made it easier to get through the divorce, both professionally as my lawyer and personally as a friend.

He didn't have that kind of support. So it's all been harder for him and I think he resents me for that and I know he resented Nancy. But still, I don't see him as someone that would ever go so far as to murder someone."

"Can you think of anyone else that might have had a motive?"

"No. I can't think of anyone. So, I guess I understand why they are at least considering Peter, if there are no other valid suspects. I hope they come up with one soon, though. I think this is taking a toll on him."

Sheila sounded convinced that Peter had nothing to do with Nancy's murder. But now, after listening to how much he'd resented Nancy's relationship with Sheila, Emma had to wonder. She'd share all of this with Mickey and her mother as they both met with Peter. As far as motives went, it was the strongest one she'd heard so far.

She and Sheila stayed and chatted over a second drink, and then Sheila had to get home.

"Peter had the kids tonight, but he's bringing them by in the morning and I can't risk a hangover."

"Two is usually my limit, too. I'm ready to call it a night."

They said their goodbyes to everyone and walked back to the office and their cars. Emma noticed that Sheila drove quite a nice car, a silver Mercedes. It looked like an older model though.

"Oh, I have a doctor's appointment in the morning on Monday, so I'll probably be in around ten or ten thirty. I'll see you then. Oh, and I have a pile of stuff for you to shred. It's right on my desk if you want to start on that. Just use the shredder in my office," Sheila said.

"Sounds good. Have a good night." Emma smiled to herself as she unlocked her car and slid into the seat. Hopefully Monday morning while Sheila was out, she'd have a chance to snoop a little in her office.

EMMA HAD A RELAXING WEEKEND. SHE HIT THE GYM ON Saturday and ran into Tess and they decided to get together on Sunday for a cookout on Emma's deck. Emma picked up a box of Bubba burgers and a package of hot dogs and Tess brought over chips, potato salad and a bottle of Pinot Grigio.

Oscar hung out with them at a distance and went scurrying off when Hayley got excited and ran over to pet him.

"I didn't realize you got a cat. Hayley loves animals. I think her excitement scares them a little though," Tess said.

"He's a stray that kept coming around and then stayed. He's very sweet, but maybe a little skittish around children, it seems."

Tess poured them each a glass of wine, while Emma put the burgers and dogs on the grill. Once everything was ready, they ate on the deck and caught up with each other.

"How's Brady? Has he been around much?" Tess asked.

"He travels a lot, but we went for a bite last Friday, to Fisherman's View in Sandwich. It was really good. Have you been there?"

Tess nodded. "It's great. One of my favorite places. Was that a date?"

Emma laughed. "It was so not a date. Not at all. Just two neighbors sharing a meal. I think Brady could be a good friend. It's nice having someone I know nearby."

"I'm pretty sure he's single. Just saying."

"He is. We talked about that. I think we're good the way things are. My brother doesn't approve of him, anyway. Not that I agree with that."

"He doesn't? Why not?"

"I'm not really sure, but he said it's something to do with the last girl he dated seriously, Caroline, someone. She was a friend of my brother's and he didn't like the way Brady ended things. But I told Matt that we only know Caroline's side of the story."

"That's true. I vaguely remember hearing about that. It was a while ago. I don't remember the details. It will come to me though. Caroline goes to the gym too and is friendly with one of the other trainers, so we talked about it back then."

"So, what about you? Are you dating anyone?" Emma asked.

Tess's face lit up. "Actually, I am. We've gone out twice now. I met Brian at the gym—shocker, right? He's also divorced and has a boy about Hayley's age. So we have a lot in common. I think we both want to take it slow though."

"That's great, and smart."

"Yeah, everyone seems great at first. You need to really get to know someone to see the real person. But, so far, I like what I've seen."

Emma told her about drinks Friday night with the law firm and about Justin's new yacht.

Tess laughed. "I'm so not surprised that he has a yacht. Or that he invited you onto it. Like I've said before, that is one man that really shouldn't be married. He's such a flirt."

"He is. It sounds like his firm is being investigated now too, for some kind of Ponzi scheme. Please keep that to yourself though." It occurred to Emma after she said it that maybe that wasn't for public knowledge yet.

"No kidding? Well, that's actually not that surprising. I mean, I know lawyers do well, but multi-million dollar yachts? And a collection of expensive luxury cars? That seems over-the-top for a Plymouth lawyer."

"He's definitely larger-than-life," Emma agreed.

"How long are you temping there?"

"I just went back for a few days last week and am finishing up on Monday."

"Well, I hope you find something you can use."

"Me too."

———

THE OFFICE WAS QUIET MONDAY MORNING WHEN EMMA arrived at a quarter to eight. The office didn't officially open until nine for clients, but she knew a few people always came in early and she wanted to be one of them. The front reception desk area was empty and dark. Alyssa hadn't arrived yet, but Emma knew she'd be in shortly.

She went to her desk, which was just outside of Sheila's office and then strolled into the kitchen and made herself a coffee. There were a few attorneys in and they all had their doors closed. No other support staff had yet arrived. Emma took her coffee back to her desk and picked up her cell phone. Her plan was to quickly try to find the Sinclair folder and snap some pics of the documents to look at later.

The stack of manilla folders with papers to be shredded was right where Sheila said it would be. Emma stepped out of her office, took a look around to make sure no one was coming her way, then took a deep breath and opened Sheila's file cabinet. It was neatly organized and alphabetized, and she quickly found the S section. But the Sinclair folder wasn't there. She realized she was probably too late and Sheila had already removed the folder. That was disappointing. She slipped her phone into her pocket, opened the first folder and glanced at the papers quickly before feeding them ten at a time through the shredder.

When she was half-way through the stack of folders, something caught her eye and she looked more closely. She recognized the name—Andrew Sinclair! That's why the folder wasn't in Sheila's cabinet. Emma was supposed to shred it.

She thought about what to do. Since the papers were going to be shredded anyway, maybe she could just tuck the Sinclair ones in her purse. But that didn't feel right. And what if Sheila decided to look through the shredder material for some reason and didn't see the Sinclair documents?

So, she fished out her phone and peeked her head out of the office first to make sure no one was around. The coast was clear, so she quickly snapped pictures of all eight pages. She wasn't sure exactly what they were. She didn't have time to closely review them until later. So as soon as she was done taking the pictures, she slipped her phone back in her pocket and finished shredding.

As she went through the rest, she noticed quite a few of them had the same wording as the Sinclair documents —structured settlements. She snapped a few more pictures here and there, mostly the first and last pages that had signatures on them, which would indicate which attorneys worked on the cases. She finished about a half hour before Sheila was due to be in. She'd just sat back at her desk and before diving into the day's typing was going to look through some of her images on her phone. But just as Emma reached for her phone, she heard someone coming down the hall and looked up.

Sheila smiled. "I finished up sooner than expected. How'd the shredding go?"

"It's done. I was just about to dive into some typing."

"Great, thanks so much."

Emma didn't have a chance to look at her phone until lunchtime. She left the office and walked over to Chipotle, ordered some loaded tofu tacos and sat on a stool facing a window. She took one bite of her taco, then pulled open her phone and started closely reviewing the documents she'd copied.

Like the Sinclair documents, they were all structured settlements and all of them had three signatures on them —Justin, Sheila and Nancy. Emma wasn't sure what that meant, but it looked to her as though Nancy may have been involved in Justin's schemes. And maybe it was that involvement that got her killed?

CHAPTER 18

When Emma got into the office Tuesday morning, she sent the pictures from her phone to her computer and printed out the documents. She'd called her mother on the way home from the law office the night before and filled her in. They agreed to discuss with Mickey in the morning and figure out next steps.

Emma studied the documents once they were printed out. She didn't understand the intricacies of the investment vehicle, but she did find it interesting that Justin, Sheila and Nancy's names and signatures were on all the documents. Maybe there was nothing wrong with what they were doing. Or maybe some of them didn't realize it at first.

The big question was what to do next. Technically, Emma shouldn't even have access to this information. And they still were looking at other suspects, Owen and Peter.

Mickey and Emma's mother arrived at the same time. Once they had their coffee, everyone gathered around the coffee table where Emma had the documents spread out for review. She filled them in on what they were looking at.

"So, I don't know what it all means, if anything. But Justin, Sheila, and Nancy's names are on those documents. They signed off on whatever these investment schemes are."

"Have the FBI determined that something shady is going on?" Mickey asked.

Emma's mother shook her head. "Rich said they have an investigation in process, no findings yet."

"Well, you won't like my suggestion, but I think the best thing for us to do with this information is to just turn it over to Rich and let him follow up with the FBI. If they are already investigating—they might have it. Unless they haven't turned it over to them yet. Given that Sheila had Emma shredding relevant documents, it makes you wonder."

"I'll text him now," Emma's mother said.

"Well, what can we do then?" Emma asked.

"I was thinking about that. We haven't talked to Owen's neighbors yet. Maybe they noticed something. If we can rule him in or out, that will help narrow things some."

"And Peter? Should we talk to his neighbors too?" Emma asked.

Mickey nodded. "Might as well. Now that this has all been in the paper. I like to hold off on involving neighbors until there's more to go on. Don't want to be creating suspicion unnecessarily."

"That makes sense. I wondered why we didn't do this before," Emma said.

They all turned at the sound of a knock on the door. Emma's mother jumped up and smiled when she saw who it was through the frosted glass window. She opened the door and Rich Gregory stepped in.

"That was fast. I only texted you a few minutes ago."

"I was getting a coffee at Kiskadee when I saw your text and drove right over."

"Come on in and have a seat. We were just going over everything. I'll let my daughter, Emma, tell you what she discovered."

Rich took a seat on the sofa next to Emma's mother.

"So, I sort of went undercover at the law firm where Nancy worked," Emma began.

Rich raised his eyebrows. "Undercover?"

Emma smiled nervously. "I worked a temp job there, helping the office manager with secretarial projects. While I was shredding a pile of files yesterday, I noticed that one of them was Andrew Sinclair's."

"Belinda Russell told me about the FBI investigation. I shared that with Emma and Mickey, so Emma recognized the name when she saw it."

"Okay. What did you do with it?" Rich asked.

"Well, I debated taking the file. I mean, they were going to shred it, anyway. But then I got nervous and just snapped pictures of it instead." She picked up the pages that she'd paper clipped together and handed them to

Rich. "Here you go. I snapped some pics of a few other documents too that looked similar in scope—about the same structured settlements investments."

Rich glanced at the papers and flipped to the last page that had the signatures. "Can I take this?"

"Of course. I wasn't sure if it could be useful to you or not—considering how it was obtained."

Rich chuckled. "Right. I can't use it directly—not yet. But I can give my contact at the FBI a heads up to look more closely in this direction. If they don't have the same paper files, they can demand electronic ones."

"Thank you. We weren't sure if there was much we could do with it, so Mickey suggested sharing it with you. Take the others as well." Emma scooped up all the documents and handed them to Rich.

"We were going to have a chat with Owen Sturgess's neighbors today if we can, and also with Peter's. Unless you've already done that and learned anything worthwhile?" Mickey asked.

"Our guys talked to Peter's neighbors yesterday, and he's officially no longer a suspect. One of them saw him during the window of time he would have been killing Nancy. I'm not surprised. I never saw him as the killer," Rich said.

Mickey nodded. "Okay, we'll just follow up with Owen's neighbors then. You haven't talked to them?"

"We talked to one of them, but didn't get anywhere. They said they couldn't remember anything."

"All right. We'll see what we come up with then. Maybe their memories will be better today."

Rich stood. "Good luck. Please keep me posted if you do learn anything." He turned to Emma's mother. "I have to head out. Are we still on for dinner on Thursday?"

"Yes, that still works for me," her mother said.

Rich broke into a smile that lit up his whole face. "Great. I'll talk to you in a few days then."

Emma's mother walked Rich to the door and when she returned to the sofa she was wearing a goofy, silly smile. Her mother was totally smitten. It was cute to see.

Mickey meanwhile had looked up the neighbors on either side of Owen and called them both. One didn't pick up, so he left a message. The other, an older woman named Agatha Riddle, answered on the first ring and told them to stop by anytime.

"All right. Are you ready to head out, Emma?"

"I'm ready!"

"Good luck, you two. I'm off to teach a yoga class, but I'll be online later and checking messages. Keep me posted."

It was a beautiful day with no wind at all, so Mickey insisted on driving. Emma pulled her hair into a ponytail and hopped into the passenger side of Mickey's convertible. Fifteen minutes later, they turned left onto Emerson Road in the Priscilla Beach neighborhood. They followed the road until it ended on Priscilla Beach Road which faced the ocean. Owen's house was immediately to the right, and they drove past it and parked in the driveway of his neighbor, Agatha Riddle.

She heard them drive up and was standing in the doorway holding it open for them to come in.

Once the polite introductions were made, Agatha led them into her sitting room, which faced the ocean, and on the side, looked out over Owen's house.

"Call me Aggie. Would either of you like a nice hot cup of tea?"

"No, thank you," Emma said automatically.

But Mickey nodded. "Only if you're having a cup. I don't want to be any trouble."

Aggie smiled. "Oh, no trouble at all. I made a big pot of hot water. Are you sure you don't want a cup, young lady?"

"All right, I'll join you. Thank you. Can I help?"

"Why don't you come with me, dear. You can help me carry it all."

Emma followed the older woman into her kitchen, which was quite modern and spotless. Sure enough, an electric tea kettle was full of steaming hot water, which Aggie poured into three delicate china teacups. She added the tea bags and put all the cups and saucers on a tray along with a jar of sugar packets and a tiny pitcher of milk. She handed Emma a big plate of chocolate chip cookies.

"I just baked those yesterday. They're still quite good, if I do say so myself."

Emma carried the cookies out to where Mickey was sitting and put them on the table in front of him. His eyes lit up when he saw them. Aggie followed with her tray and set everything on the table. Once they were all settled with cups of tea and a cookie in hand, Aggie smiled and invited them to ask their questions.

"I don't miss much in this neighborhood. This is my usual spot and sitting here I can see everything down on the beach as well as what my neighbors are up to. Usually it's not very interesting, but you never do know."

Emma took a bite of her cookie. "Oh, these are delicious."

Aggie beamed. "Thank you, dear. I'd say it was a secret recipe, but I'd be lying. I just use the one on the chocolate chip bag—Toll House cookies. It's the best."

"I agree," Mickey said. "So, we're here on behalf of Nancy Eldridge's mother, Belinda. Nancy was the woman who was recently murdered. She'd arrived home around seven and was never seen again. We are looking into all kinds of avenues, but we're curious if you happened to notice if Owen Sturgess was home the evening of the murder."

Aggie thought for a moment. "What day was it again?"

Mickey told her the exact date, and added, "It was a Thursday."

Aggie stared out the window at Owen's house and then smiled and turned back to face them.

"So, I'm not a fan of his. I don't much care for his funny business while he was married. I'm glad Claire is divorcing him. But he was definitely home that night. He left a little after five and was back less than an hour later with that young woman he's dating. She had a suitcase with her. They didn't leave the house the rest of the night. I think he must have picked her up at the bus station."

"You're sure it was that day?" Emma asked.

Aggie nodded. "It was definitely a Thursday because I was watching my show. That Bobby Flay chef show, it's on every Thursday at six. It was just starting when they got home."

Mickey closed his notepad.

"I think that's all we need, then. Thank you so much for your time."

"Oh, it was my pleasure. Stay and relax a bit. Have another cookie or two."

Mickey didn't need to be asked twice. He reached for another cookie and Emma did the same. They stayed and chatted with Aggie for another twenty minutes or so and then headed back to the office.

As soon as they got in the car, Mickey spoke. "Well, that clears Owen then. Too bad, I wouldn't have minded if it was him."

Emma laughed. "I was thinking the same thing."

As they were driving back to the office, Emma's cell phone rang, and she was surprised to see that it was Tess. She didn't usually hear from her during the day.

"Hey, Tess, what's up?"

"So, I'm at work and this is kind of weird. I just checked Brady in for a workout and glanced at his recent check ins. He came to the gym the day that Nancy was murdered. I thought you'd said he was out of town?"

"I thought that's what he said, too. That he was away then."

"Well, not according to the computer. It looks like he came Sunday morning and then not again until Thursday. So he probably got home the night before."

"Thanks, Tess. We'll look into this. I could have sworn he said he didn't get home until the next day."

"Right. It just kind of jumped out at me and I thought you should know. Hopefully, there's nothing to it. Keep me posted."

"I will. Thanks, Tess."

CHAPTER 19

When Emma got home, she noticed Brady's car was there. It had been gone for the last few days, and she assumed he was away for business. It was only a quarter past five and she was starting to get hungry. There was also nothing in her house that she wanted to eat. She needed to go grocery shopping and didn't particularly feel like doing that either at the moment.

A loud meow got her attention, and she saw Oscar sitting on her deck waiting for her to let him in. She opened the door, went to the kitchen and put some food in a bowl for him. He pounced on it and she gave him a quick scratch behind the ears before pouring herself a glass of water and stepping outside on the deck.

Even though it was late in the day, the beach was crowded with people walking, swimming and chatting in small groups. A group of teenagers were building a bonfire. Emma glanced over at Brady's house and thought about what Tess said. There had to be a good explanation for why Brady hadn't mentioned that he was in town the day Nancy died.

Her stomach growled as she sipped her water and debated what to do. Brady stepped out onto his deck, saw her and waved. She took a deep breath and made a decision.

"Hey Brady. I'm thinking about going to Leena's Kitchen for dinner tonight. Any interest in joining me?"

He looked delighted by the invitation. A slow grin lit up his face.

"Sure. I love Leena's Kitchen. I'm ready when you are."

"Okay, give me five minutes and we can head out."

Emma freshened up and added a swipe of lipstick before stepping outside. She was going to walk to Brady's and knock on his door, but she didn't have to. She took one step in his direction and his front door opened.

"I can drive, unless you'd rather?" he said when he reached her.

"I don't mind driving." She preferred it actually, as she felt more in control and only planned to have one glass of wine, if that. She could sip it slowly so that Brady might be encouraged to have a few drinks, and when he was good and relaxed, she could slide some questions in.

"Leena's is one of my mother's favorite places. Mine too, actually," Brady said as they got into Emma's car. They chatted about nothing in particular as Emma drove, and fifteen minutes later, she turned into the parking lot of the strip mall where Leena's Kitchen was located.

They were there early, and it wasn't too crowded yet. The host led them to a cozy table in a corner. A moment later, a server came by to take their drinks order and tell them the specials.

"Do you want to split a bottle of wine?" Brady suggested. "I usually drink beer but I like wine with Italian food and they have some good ones here."

"Sure. I was planning on getting wine."

"Have you had the J Vineyards? My mother and I had that last time we were here, and it was good."

Emma smiled. "I love that one. That's what I usually get here too, and it's funny as I don't normally drink Pinot Noir."

Their server returned with the wine, opened the bottle, and poured a small sip for Brady to taste. He tossed it back and smiled. "Delicious, thank you."

The server filled Emma's glass and then Brady's. They put their order in—Emma went with the lobster gnocchi and Brady got one of the specials, a braised lamb shank. They both got Caesar salads to start, which came out just a few minutes later with a hot and crusty small loaf of bread.

"This is the best Caesar in Plymouth," Emma said as she took her first bite. The croutons were like little pillows of French toast, crispy on the outside and soft in the middle.

"I would have to agree with that," Brady said as he reached for a slice of bread and spread a thick layer of butter on it. Emma dipped hers in the dish of seasoned olive oil.

"So, how was your week? Where did you fly off to this time?" Emma asked.

"San Francisco. For one of my tech clients in Silicon Valley."

"I visited San Francisco when I lived in L.A. Went for a long weekend with one of my girlfriends. We rented a car and drove to wine country, toured a few of the vineyards. I wouldn't mind going back there and spending more time exploring. I liked the whole vibe of San Francisco. It's very different from L.A."

"It is. I've been to L.A. a few times and am not really a fan. San Francisco is awesome, though. So many great restaurants there. I get out that way once or twice a quarter as I have a few clients on the West Coast."

The wine was so good that Emma had to remind herself to sip it slowly. When their meals came, her glass was still mostly full and Brady's was almost empty. She picked up the wine bottle and refilled his glass almost to the brim and then added a small splash to hers.

"Thanks!"

Their meals were excellent, as usual, and Brady kept her entertained with funny stories about some of his clients. When they were done, Emma packed up her leftovers and Brady had eaten every last crumb.

"You know, Leena's has the best tiramisu on the South Shore. Any interest in sharing a slice?" Emma asked.

"Sure, why not?"

Once again, Emma topped off his glass, which was almost empty and added the smallest of splashes to hers.

"So, how was your week?" Brady asked when the server returned with their dessert and two forks.

Emma picked up a fork, took a bite, and then answered the question.

"It was good, but frustrating. We're really no closer to finding out what happened to Nancy. We keep going back over everything."

"The police aren't getting any closer either?" Brady asked.

Emma shook her head. "Not really. They are looking in a few different directions but don't have anything solid yet."

"Wish I could do something to help. Still can't believe she's gone."

"Looking back, does anything else come to mind? You guys used to work out together a few times a week. Did you see her that week at all?"

"No, not that week. I had a tough travel schedule. I was gone Sunday and home Wednesday night, then flew back out for an overnight trip Thursday night. I did go to the gym on Thursday, but I didn't even call Nancy as I had such a tight window. I went to the gym, showered, changed and left from there straight to the airport for a two o'clock flight to New York."

Emma relaxed a little. If what Brady said was true, that meant he wasn't around when Nancy disappeared. That was good news. She liked Brady and couldn't picture him being involved in Nancy's disappearance.

When the check came, Brady tried to pay, but Emma insisted that they split it.

"That's very nice of you, but I can pay my own way. That's what friends do."

Brady smiled. "Sometimes friends just want to treat too, though."

Emma laughed. "Another time, maybe."

They finished up and Emma felt very full and relaxed as she drove home. She knew she'd probably fall asleep as soon as her head hit the pillow. Pasta often had that effect on her.

When they reached their cottages, Brady walked her to her door.

"I'm glad you suggested dinner tonight, Emma. That was fun. We should make a habit of it."

She smiled. "I agree." And as she closed and locked the door behind her, she felt a sense of relief that she didn't have to worry about Brady anymore. She'd never really thought he was involved and the more she got to know him, the more she enjoyed his company.

THE NEXT MORNING, OVER COFFEE IN THE OFFICE, EMMA filled her mother and Mickey in on her conversation with Brady. They didn't share her enthusiasm.

"I don't like that you went off alone with him in a car," Mickey said.

"I don't either. Did you have to go to dinner with him? You couldn't have just had a conversation—ideally with each of you on your own decks?" Her mother said.

Emma looked at both of them in frustration. "I'm not

sure if you both heard me. Brady's in the clear. He wasn't here."

"So he says," Mickey said.

Her mother nodded. "You don't know that he's telling the truth, honey. He might just be trying to cover something up. Or he might be perfectly fine, but right now you just have his word."

Emma agreed that they did have a point. "So, how do we go about verifying his flight information?"

"Well, short of asking him for copies of his boarding passes, you can't," Mickey said. "But the police can. They can access flight and passenger records and could confirm if what he's saying is true."

"I'll call Rich." Emma's mother went to get her phone and made a quick call before rejoining them.

"He said he'll look into it. He said they never considered Brady a suspect, but it's still an open investigation so they are eager to pursue every lead."

"Nothing new on the law firm shenanigans?" Mickey asked.

"He said no, not yet. He also said that even if they prove there was some kind of fraud or criminal activity within the firm, that doesn't necessarily prove a connection to Nancy's death."

"No. But it seems like the best place to dig around," Emma said.

"That's true," Mickey said.

"On a different note, I heard from Claire Sturgess on my way in today. She said to thank you both. What you uncovered on Owen helped her case quite a bit. She still has to pay him alimony, but it's not as bad as she'd feared initially."

"Oh, that is good news," Emma said.

Her mother checked her notebook before updating them. "We have a new case you can start on today too. A Bryan Filmore suspects that his wife is cheating on him. Interestingly, she's a junior attorney at of all places, the law firm Nancy worked at."

"He thinks she's cheating on him? We don't see that too often," Mickey said.

"What's her name?" Emma asked.

"Ashley. She mostly focuses on real estate law."

Emma tried to picture who Ashley was. When she covered for Alyssa, the receptionist, she saw most of the people that worked in the firm as they went in and out for lunch. Finally, it came to her. Ashley was very pretty, petite and had a trendy blond bob. Emma guessed her age to be late twenties.

"We can head over there around eleven thirty and see where she goes off to for lunch," Mickey suggested.

They spent the rest of the morning doing some computer work on a skip-tracing case. At eleven thirty sharp, Emma and Mickey stepped out the front door. Mickey had parked his car on Main Street, right across the street by the bank, Rockland Trust. He explained that when he'd arrived, the parking lot in the back of the building had been full.

Traffic on Main Street was busy, as usual, so they had to wait a few minutes before they could cross. Emma noticed the car in front of Mickey's looked familiar. It was a gorgeous older model silver Mercedes. Where had she recently seen a car like that?

It came to her at the same time she saw Sheila from the law office and a handsome, dark-haired man walking toward them. They were both holding pizza takeout boxes from The Artisan Pig, the new pizza hotspot that was a quick walk from the office. Sheila stopped short when she reached them and Emma knew they were waiting for the traffic to clear so they could cross the street too, as it was her car parked in front of Mickey's.

"Emma, what a surprise seeing you here." Sheila glanced at the door to their office and the sign that said Court Street Investigations and then back to Emma and Mickey. "A surprise seeing you both, actually."

CHAPTER 20

Emma swallowed nervously and thought hard, and finally an idea came to her. She smiled big. "Sheila, great to see you! You remember Mickey? He came in to visit when I covered the reception desk. We got to chatting and he let me know about an opening here. I just started as the new office manager!"

Sheila smiled back and seemed happy for her. "Oh, that's great! You did such a good job for us, I was actually going to request you again, but of course you want a full-time job." She glanced at the man standing next to her. "This is my boyfriend, George Montgomery. Today is our one-year anniversary, so we decided to take a long lunch and get some pizza to eat down by the waterfront."

"Happy Anniversary."

"Nice to see you again, Sheila," Mickey said.

"Well, we're off. Enjoy the rest of your day." Sheila and George headed to their car, and Mickey and Emma watched as they pulled out and took a left to head down to the waterfront.

"The Artisan Pig's pizza really is good," Emma said wistfully.

"We don't have time to get pizza. But Betty packed tuna subs and chips for us," Mickey said as he pulled onto the street, turned around in the church parking lot and headed the opposite way, to Resnik Road and the law firm.

At a quarter to twelve, they pulled into the law firm parking lot and parked far enough away that they wouldn't be noticed but where they would still have a view of the door and people coming and going. Emma opened the two bottled waters that she'd brought and handed one to Mickey. He opened his lunch bag and handed her a sub and a small bag of sour cream and onion potato chips.

They munched happily as they kept an eye on the door.

"It's funny, I don't remember Sheila mentioning that she had a boyfriend. But, maybe she did. They looked cute together. She seemed excited about their one-year anniversary," Emma said.

"When did she get divorced? Didn't think it was all that long ago," Mickey said.

Emma thought for a moment. "I think it was a little over a year. I remember Sheila said it dragged on for almost that long before it was final too."

"I'm glad I never had to go through that. Betty and I will be celebrating fifty-five years together in December."

"Wow. That's wonderful." Emma couldn't imagine being with someone that long. It sounded amazing to be happily married for so long, though.

"Yep, I knew she was the one on our third date. We both ordered the same flavor of ice-cream, black raspberry. I knew she was a keeper. Told my mother when I got home from my date that I'd found the girl for me. We got engaged six months later."

"That's so special, Mickey."

"She was twenty-three and a dance instructor, taught ballet. I'd just graduated from the police academy and started at the Plymouth Police Department. Those were the days. We were active members of the Plymouth Yacht Club. I had a little motorboat we used to tool around the harbor in. And we'd go to all the events and dances. My wife is still a fabulous dancer." He smiled, remembering. "We don't cut the rug as often as we used to. But I still have the moves, as you young people say."

Emma chuckled. "I bet you do. That sounds really fun."

They were just finishing up their subs when the front door opened. It was twelve o'clock sharp and the first employees began streaming out. Alyssa the receptionist was first, followed by an attorney that Emma didn't recognize. A moment later, though, two familiar faces walked out together—Ashley, the young attorney they were waiting for, and Justin Powell himself. Emma assumed it was a coincidence that they happened to walk out at the same time, but she was then surprised to see them both walk to Justin's black Mercedes sedan. Ashley climbed into the passenger side and a moment later, Justin backed the car out of the spot and onto the Main Street.

Mickey followed close behind.

"It might not mean anything," Emma said.

"That's true. They could just be going to lunch. Maybe they're discussing a case or something."

They followed them onto the highway and drove two exits south in Plymouth and exited onto Long Pond drive. They took a right at the lights into the Home Depot plaza.

"Maybe they're having lunch at the 99 Restaurant," Emma guessed.

But instead of turning right to go to the 99, Justin turned left towards Home Depot.

Mickey chuckled. "Something tells me they're not going shopping for new fixtures." Sure enough, Justin took another left and pulled into the parking lot for the Hilton Garden hotel.

"This looks familiar," Emma said. It was the same hotel they'd ended up at on an earlier suspected cheater case.

"A convenient location for a mid-day rendezvous," Mickey confirmed.

They watched as Justin parked and a moment later, Ashley got out of the car and walked into the hotel alone.

"That's weird. Why isn't Justin going with her?" Emma asked.

"They're being careful. He's more well-known than she is. She's getting the room or maybe he already reserved one and she's checking in. Then she'll go to her room and text him. In less than five minutes he'll be heading in, you wait and see."

Mickey rustled around in his bag and pulled out two brownies and handed one to Emma. "Betty sent these too. She said they're healthy brownies made with black beans or something. I was skeptical, but they're pretty darned good."

Emma glanced at the brownie. It looked like a normal fudgy brownie. "Black beans? Really?"

"That's what she said. Tastes the same to me."

Emma took a bite and had to agree. "Well, I guess I approve of these healthy brownies then."

"Look, he's on the move."

Justin got out of the car, looked around, and then headed into the hotel.

"So, now we just wait, right?" Emma said.

"Yep. We probably have time if you feel like running and getting us a couple of coffees, my treat?" he suggested.

Emma laughed. "I'll go get them, but you don't need to treat. You just gave me lunch."

"Well, I didn't want to be rude and just ask you to go get them."

"I don't mind. I'll be right back." Emma walked across the parking lot to the convenience store at the gas station where there was a Dunkin' Donuts inside. She returned a few minutes later with two hot coffees and sugar packets. Mickey liked his with plenty of cream and sugar. Emma preferred hers black, but sometimes in the afternoon, she slipped in a little sugar. She stirred a bit into hers and inhaled deeply before taking a sip. Something about the smell of a Dunkin' Donuts coffee. It almost smelled better than it tasted.

They chatted and sipped their coffees, and about forty-five minutes later, Justin and Ashley walked out of the hotel together. Emma thought they'd just get into his car, but Justin was apparently feeling daring. He looked in both directions, glancing right over their car, and seemed to think no one was watching. He pulled Ashley in for a passionate kiss before she pushed him away and looked around nervously. They both climbed into his car and drove off. Emma got plenty of shots.

"So, where to now? Do we follow them back to the law office?" she asked.

Mickey shook his head. "No, we got everything we need. Ashley is most definitely being unfaithful to her husband. And among other potential shenanigans, we know that Justin isn't going to win any husband of the year awards, either."

CHAPTER 21

C indy looked forward to her date with Rich all week. It had been a long time since she'd felt that kind of anticipation, the thrill of seeing a new crush. They decided to have an early dinner at Mallebar Brasserie, Plymouth's only French restaurant, which was at the beginning of Main Street. Cindy had been there once with Lee and Rachel when it first opened and they'd all loved it. The menu was very French, with rich cream sauces and elegant cocktails. Cindy looked forward to having the lobster bisque again. It was the best she'd ever had with a whole lightly fried lobster tail in the thick, sherry-laced cream.

After dinner, they walked up and down Main Street, popping into several art shops and galleries that were having an 'art crawl' open house kind of thing. There was a good crowd of people strolling along Main Street, and Cindy even found a small painting that she bought to hang in the office.

They decided to stop for an after dinner coffee at Keegan's Kreations, a pastry shop on Main Street. They walked a few yards to the Town Hall square and sat on a bench there, and people watched as they sipped their coffee.

They hadn't discussed the case at all over dinner. Which was nice, as it gave Cindy a chance to learn more about Rich. He'd told her his golf game was improving and asked if she'd had a chance to actually get on the course and play a round yet.

"Not yet. But Lee has us booked for a tee time on Sunday. I'm looking forward to it, but am a little nervous too."

"You'll be fine. It's a beautiful course at the Pinehills. You'll love it."

Finally, while they were sitting there and there was a lull in conversation, Cindy gave in to her curiosity and asked about the case.

"Any updates on Nancy's case? Or on the law firm investigation?"

Rich shook his head. "No. It's a bit frustrating. I haven't heard anything from the FBI, just that they are still looking into things. And truthfully, we're no further ahead on Nancy's investigation either. None of our leads have really panned out. We have ruled out Owen and Sheila's husband.

And it looks like Brady's story checks out. He did fly out of town the afternoon that Nancy died. So, we're kind of back to square one, unless something turns up with the law firm, but that seems like it may be unrelated. It's a little discouraging."

Cindy nodded. "I don't know if this helps any, but Justin Powell is certainly guilty of cheating. We have been working on an infidelity case and the husband of one of the attorneys there thought she was having an affair and asked us to look into it. He was correct. It turned out the person she was having the affair with was her boss, Justin Powell. He gets around."

Rich chuckled. "That's interesting. But probably unrelated."

"I agree. But, that's all we have, too. We're continuing to dig though and see what else we can come up with."

"You know, there's always the possibility that it was a random killing. That Nancy didn't know her killer."

Cindy frowned. "Do you think that's likely? I thought victims almost always knew their killers?"

"They do, usually. But not always. Sometimes bad things just happen for no apparent reason."

It was a chilling thought and Cindy found herself shivering even though it wasn't cold out. It was more reassuring to think Nancy knew her killer instead of it being a stranger. Because if it was random, that meant anyone could be in danger if this person wasn't found. And Cindy had always thought of Plymouth as such a safe place to live.

"If it is unrelated, a random killing as you say, that means it will be harder to solve?" Cindy asked.

"More challenging," Rich confirmed. "But, not

impossible. Mistakes are always made. We just need to find them. And we will."

CHAPTER 22

"Emma, I have a hankering for peppermint stick ice cream. Want to take a ride with me to Gellar's?" It was hard to say no to Mickey.

Emma drove by Gellar's every day on her way home. It was where she turned left off of Route 3A to reach Taylor Avenue and the beach. But she hadn't stopped there for ice cream since she'd been back. Gellar's sold everything she usually tried to avoid—ice cream, hot dogs, burgers, and fried seafood.

But she was feeling a little stir crazy after being on the computer all morning as she and Mickey worked on a new skip-tracing case. It was a beautiful day, and she'd only had a salad for lunch, so she agreed to go.

Mickey drove his convertible and when they reached Gellar's, there was a short line of children and parents waiting to order. They took their place and didn't have to wait too long. Mickey got a cone with peppermint stick ice cream, and Emma splurged on a small hot fudge sundae with whipped cream and nuts. They ate at a small picnic table. Emma had her phone next to her and when they were almost done eating, a text message came through from Tess.

Nice article in today's Patriot Ledger. Great picture of you all.

Emma had no idea what she was talking about.

"Mickey, do you know anything about an article in the paper on us?"

He shook his head. "Nope. We can stop and pick up a paper on the way back to the office though."

When they left Gellar's, Mickey drove across the street to the Seven Eleven convenience store and Emma ran in and bought a paper. While Mickey drove back to the office, she flipped through the paper until she found the article Tess was taking about. It wasn't an article so much as a press release. And since Mickey knew nothing about it, she figured her mother must have sent it in. She wasn't in the office, so Emma called her.

"Hi, honey. I only have a minute or two before my class starts. What's going on?"

"Did you send a press release into the paper? There's something on us in this week's Patriot Ledger, with a picture and everything."

"Really? I sent that in to them so long ago. I didn't think they were going to run it. Remember when we first visited the office and met with Mickey—before you moved back? Betty was there and snapped the picture of the three of us."

Emma did remember.

"I didn't realize you sent anything in to the paper."

"I did it before you were even back, honey. Just as an announcement, to try to get the word out. Does it look nice?"

Emma laughed. "It does. But, it kind of blows my cover. I ran into Sheila the other day as Mickey and I left the office. I told her I just started working here. She seemed to believe me. But, if she sees this... I guess it doesn't really matter."

"I wouldn't worry about it, honey. I have to run. See you in the morning."

Emma supposed it was good public relations for the agency, but it made her a little uneasy. When they got back to the office, she looked up both Sheila and her new boyfriend in Tracers, their database, to see if either of them had any kind of criminal record.

Mickey raised his eyebrows when he walked by her computer and saw what she was doing.

"I don't think you have anything to worry about. They probably don't even read that paper," Mickey said.

"Probably not," Emma agreed. She never read it. It was a local paper, and she hadn't bought an actual print paper in years. She just read her news online, often after seeing a headline on Facebook, and she had a daily recap of breaking news emailed to her.

Mickey was curious, though, to see what she found. "So, any priors for either of them?"

Emma looked up Sheila first and there was nothing there. She was squeaky clean. Her boyfriend, George, though, was a different story.

"Hmmm. This is interesting. There's nothing on Sheila, but I didn't expect that there would be. Her boyfriend though—Well I wonder if she knows about his background?"

"Yeah? How bad is it?"

"Two charges of aggravated assault. Looks like he used to work as a bouncer and took the job a little too seriously. Maybe not as bad as it seems."

"Recently?" Mickey asked.

"No, it was almost ten years ago."

"Is he still a bouncer?"

"No, looks like he drives a delivery truck for a local food supply business."

"So, maybe he settled down, now that he's a little older," Mickey said. "Doesn't sound like we have to worry about those two."

Emma sighed. "No, you're probably right. If anyone at the law firm is involved in Nancy's death, it's probably Justin—if he really is running some kind of illegal scheme. Sheila is just the office manager, so she might not even know the extent of it."

Mickey nodded. "Right, and like your mother said, Rich told her the FBI doesn't even know if there's any kind of connection between that case and Nancy's death. They might be completely unrelated."

"Do you think there's a possibility that Nancy's death was completely random?" Her mother had told them about her conversation with Rich, and the possibility that there was no motive at all. It was a scary thought.

But Mickey shook his head. "It's possible. But it's highly doubtful. Random murders rarely happen."

"I feel like we are back at square one. Unless it turns out there is some connection with the law firm Ponzi scheme. Too bad I can't go back in and temp again."

"Right. Unfortunately, that door is closed. I don't suppose I could get Justin to agree to talk to me again."

Emma smiled, remembering a comment Tess had made a while back. "Maybe I can get him to talk to me."

Mickey frowned. "I don't think it's a good idea for you to go back to that law firm."

"I agree. But I was thinking I'd go to Sushi Joy. Tess said Justin is there almost every Thursday night. I can order some food to go and have a drink at the bar."

Mickey looked doubtful. "Maybe I should go with you?"

Emma smiled. "I'd love your company, but I think it might be better if I go alone. I'll be perfectly safe at Sushi Joy."

CHAPTER 23

E mma arrived at Sushi Joy at a quarter to four on Thursday. She remembered that Tess had said that Justin usually arrived by four or so. His black Mercedes wasn't out front yet when Emma parked, but she figured he'd be along shortly. It was early still, before the dinner rush and the bar was empty except for an older gentleman who was paying his bill. Emma scanned the bar, which had about a dozen or so seats along one side and four on the short side. She decided to sit somewhere in the middle.

She settled into a bar seat and set her phone on the bar. A bartender came right over and she ordered a glass of chardonnay and looked over a menu. She always ordered the same thing when she went there—spicy tuna over seaweed salad and a Godzilla roll which was shrimp, tuna, avocado and ginger in a roll that was lightly deep fried. It was ridiculously delicious.

She decided to wait a bit to put her order in though

and sipped her wine as if she was having a hard time deciding. At four o'clock sharp, the front door opened, and she recognized Justin's cheerful, booming voice as he said hello to the girls at the hostess stand before stepping into the bar area. He looked around and smiled when he recognized Emma. He was by himself and sat in the chair on her left.

"Well, hello there. Happy Thursday. Emily, right?"

Emma smiled. "Close. Emma."

Justin laughed. "Of course. Good to see you, Emma. Did you already eat?"

"No, I was going to order some food to go."

"Don't do that. Unless you have to hurry off somewhere. I'm going to order some food too. We can keep each other company."

Emma didn't hesitate. "Sure, I can do that."

The bartender came over and set down Justin's martini with extra olives. He didn't even have to order it.

"How's that for service, Emma? Caitlin is the best." He beamed at the bartender, who smiled back enthusiastically. Emma suspected that the enthusiasm was because Justin was a good tipper.

"Are you ordering your usual?" Caitlin asked.

He nodded. "Yes. Peking ravioli, Kiss the Fire and a Godzilla roll, and whatever this lovely lady would like." He glanced at Emma, and she quickly put her order in.

"What's a Kiss the Fire roll?" Emma hadn't tried that one before.

"Oh, it's great. Shrimp and avocado topped with two

kinds of sliced fresh tuna and a sliver of jalapeño. You'll have to try it. I always order too much food."

The bar began to fill up as people streamed in, and many of them knew Justin and stopped by to say hello. It didn't take long for their food to come out, and once it did, he turned his attention to that and to Emma.

"Try a piece of the Kiss the Fire," he insisted. She did, and it was wonderful. Almost as good as the Godzilla roll.

She pondered how to get Justin to talk about the firm.

"How's everything at the firm? Busy as ever?" she finally asked.

"Oh, yeah. Business is booming. Busier than ever," he said proudly.

"That's great. A shame they still don't seem to have any idea what happened to Nancy Eldridge. I just read an update today that it sounds like they are back to square one."

Justin looked surprised. "Really? Back to square one. That's disappointing. I'd hoped they'd be closing in on someone by now."

He seemed sincere. So unless he was a really good actor, Emma didn't think he was involved in Nancy's death. But then she remembered what Mickey said about Ted Bundy. How no-one ever suspected him either, because he was so charming.

"Sheila said that everyone liked Nancy. So, who would have a reason to kill her?" she wondered aloud.

Justin looked serious for the first time. "That's what I

kept saying too. I still don't understand it. She was a great girl."

"Sheila said they were best friends, and it just didn't make any sense. She couldn't think of anyone that would have a motive either. Maybe it was just a random thing?"

"Sheila said they were best friends? I didn't realize they were that close. Ever since she started dating that guy George, she's been spending most of her time with him. I think she and Nancy were pretty good friends, but just not as close as they used to be. I guess that's what happens when a new guy comes along, right?"

Emma smiled. "That's probably true." She knew lots of girls that dropped their friends as soon as they got serious with a new guy. It was something Emma tried not to do, as she'd been on the receiving end of it, and it was annoying when friends canceled plans to go out with their latest date instead. She understood if it was a onetime thing, but when it happened repeatedly, it was irritating.

"So, what about you, Emma? Are you seeing anyone?" The question had a flirtatious tone to it, and Emma was regretting that she hadn't gotten her food to go. Justin was nice enough, but she would never be interested in a married man, or someone that much older. She knew plenty of women were, though.

"I am dating someone," she lied.

"Of course you are. If it's not serious though, you really should come to my next boat party. We're taking her out Sunday afternoon for a later afternoon harbor cruise. Stop down around three if you want to join us. It will be a blast."

"It sounds fun. I'll keep it in mind," she said. She finished her tuna on seaweed salad and packed up half of her Godzilla roll to finish later. She rarely was hungry enough to finish both in one sitting. Emma asked the bartender for her check when she came to check on them.

"There is no check. You're on Justin's tab."

Emma turned to Justin. "You don't have to buy my dinner. Let me give you some money for that. She reached in her purse and he shook his head.

"Your money is no good here. You agreed to keep me company, and it was my pleasure."

Emma felt awkward. "Well, thank you then. That's very nice of you."

He laughed. "Have a good night, Emma. And remember, Sunday at three if you want to have a blast with us. It will be a good time."

"I'll keep that in mind. Goodnight, Justin."

CHAPTER 24

I t was still light out when Emma got home. The sun was just beginning to set, and the sky was a rosy pink. Oscar was waiting for her, and she let him in and gave him a small can of wet food. He was beginning to fill out nicely. She put her leftovers in the refrigerator, grabbed a bottled water and stepped out on the deck.

She loved watching the sun set over the water. It was a relaxing time of day. The air was still, and the ocean looked like glass, barely a ripple across the surface. All was calm and serene. She sat and put her feet up on the railing, and thought about her conversation with Justin.

As much as she thought the guy was an obnoxious flirt and an obvious cheat, he was still likable, and she really found it hard to see him having anything to do with Nancy's death. Yet, at this point, he was the only one that had any kind of motive. And he did have an alibi. Rich had mentioned that he was having one of his boat parties the night that Nancy died. So, unless he hired someone to kill her, it was pretty unlikely that he was involved.

Emma still had an uneasy feeling that she was missing something. Maybe she would have her mother check with Rich to see if they ever looked at Sheila or her boyfriend, George. Though, that didn't make sense either, as Sheila had said she was Nancy's best friend. Best friends didn't kill each other. And she'd been so broken up about it, crying at the funeral and when she told Emma how close they were and how everyone loved Nancy.

So, they really were back at square one. Emma shivered as she thought about the possibility that it might have actually been a random killing. If it was, that meant anyone could be next. It could even be a serial killer. Though the idea of a serial killer in Plymouth seemed far-fetched.

Movement to her left caught her eye, and she saw Brady open the door to his slider and step out. But just as quickly, he went back inside. She guessed he forgot something and went back for it. It was starting to get darker, that twilight time when the sun hasn't quite set all the way and there's still some light left, but any moment it could be snuffed out.

It was then that she saw two familiar figures walking down the beach coming towards her. Sheila and her boyfriend George. They looked like they might have just gone out to dinner. Sheila was in a flowing orange sleeveless dress and George was in dark pants, a white dress shirt that was untucked at the waist, and the first two buttons were undone. He was holding something in his hand and Emma saw that it was a neck tie, all balled up like he'd just taken it off.

A chill ran through her. Nancy had been strangled. She looked away and quickly dialed Brady's number. He answered on the first ring.

"Hey, what's up? I was just going to come out on my deck."

"Brady, can you just listen....I might need you to come over here in a few minutes."

"What's wrong, Emma?"

"Just listen, Brady....and come over."

Emma slipped the phone in her back pocket but kept the connection live, so Brady could listen. She also hit record.

Sheila and George walked up the steps to her deck. Both of them were smiling, and it made Emma shiver again.

"So, this is where you live, Emma," Sheila said.

George looked around. "Nice place. A little small, but the view isn't bad."

"Thanks," Emma said.

"You know why we're here, don't you, Emma?" Sheila said softly.

Emma thought she did know now, but thought it best to play stupid. "No, I don't."

"You didn't just start at the PI agency. That was a lie. We saw the article in the paper. It was your father's agency."

Emma said nothing.

"Which means that you know too much, Emma. I should have done that shredding myself."

"Nancy was your best friend. How could you?" Emma said.

Sheila laughed. "Nancy was never my best friend." She smiled at George and squeezed his hand. "That was always George. Nancy was a good friend, though. She made things easier for me. I do miss that." She sounded like she missed what Nancy did for her more than she actually missed her friend.

Emma began to connect the dots. She still didn't think that Justin was involved, but now she knew that Sheila was very much aware of what was going on.

"You knew what Justin was doing. Was he giving you a cut or something?" She thought of the silver Mercedes that Sheila drove.

"He would have done the same for Nancy. His mistake was ever having her sign those first few deals. She thought they were legit at first. But she was too smart. She figured it out, and she was going to say something."

"She was going to put a stop to it, and you and Justin would both be in trouble," Emma said.

"When he offered her a cut, it just made her more determined to put a stop to it. I couldn't let that happen. The money was too good and I'll be damned if I was going to let her ruin it all."

"So you killed her?" Emma still found that hard to wrap her head around.

"Well, no, not exactly. I didn't do it. I wouldn't be able to lift her. A dead body is like dead weight, you know. Plus, she was a friend. I couldn't bring myself to do that." She smiled. "But George could." George took a step toward Emma and played with the tie in his hands. Emma took a step backwards and glanced toward Brady's house. She hadn't seen any more movement over there—it would be a good time for him to stop by.

She needed to keep Sheila talking.

"What about Nancy's phone? The police said it took a ride on the commuter rail from Kingston to South Station. That made them look at your husband, Peter. Did you do that on purpose?"

Sheila looked pleased with herself. She nodded. "Yeah, that was my idea. After George moved Nancy's body, I dropped him off at the train station and he rode to South Station and back, dropping the phone in a trash can."

"He was their top suspect for a while. You must have really hated him," Emma said.

Sheila laughed. "Oh, I don't hate Peter. He's a pain in the ass, though. I knew it wouldn't be enough to convict him, but thought it might send the police in the wrong direction for a while. And it did."

"So, what now? The FBI is investigating. They will figure this all out, eventually."

"Not if I can help it. We've gotten rid of all the evidence. Files are shredded. It should all die down soon," Sheila said.

"Did Justin know about this?" Emma asked.

"No. Justin had nothing to do with this. He never

would have done anything, and Nancy was going to bring us both down. So, I had no choice."

"So, why are you here then? Killing me isn't going to help you."

"Well, you know too much now. We don't really have a choice. It's too bad, I did like you," Sheila said. She glanced at George. "We should get this over with."

George lifted the necktie and took a step toward Emma. She was about to scramble up and over the deck and make a run for it when the door to her deck opened and Brady stepped outside, holding a gun.

"Both of you, sit," he said, directing George and Sheila to sit at the round table. George rushed at him instead and Brady shot the gun into the air and stuck his foot out at the same time, so George was disoriented and tripped.

Brady stood over him, holding the gun.

"Next time, I won't aim at the sky. Take a seat."

In the distance, Emma heard sirens. Brady kept the gun pointed at Sheila and George, who were both sitting at the round table looking pissed.

A few minutes later, there was a knock at Emma's door. She ran inside and let Rich and his partner, Rob, in. She led them to the deck, where Brady still had his gun pointed at Sheila and George. Emma filled Rich in. She pulled her phone out of her back pocket.

"I recorded the whole conversation."

Rich nodded. "We'll need that recording."

He gave Emma his email address, and she sent the recording off to him. Rich and Rob led Sheila and

George away in cuffs, and as soon as they were gone, Emma's legs suddenly felt weak and she grabbed hold of the deck railing to steady herself.

Brady noticed and walked over to her. "Are you okay?"

She nodded and was horrified when her eyes suddenly welled up, and she shivered.

"Come here." Brady pulled her close and hugged her tight. "You're safe. I'm right here. I'll stay here tonight if you want?"

Emma shook her head. "Thanks. I'm okay though. It was just the shock of it all hitting me. Did you hear everything?"

He nodded. "As clear as day. I wanted to come out sooner, but you still had her talking and she was burying herself. Crazy to think she could have her friend killed."

"She didn't want the money to stop. Justin must have been giving her a nice cut. I thought it was strange that an office manager was driving a high end Mercedes. Her car was gorgeous."

"You just never know about people, I guess. But, Emma, if you need anything at all, I'm right next door."

CHAPTER 25

Emma and Mickey had both been pretty good lately about avoiding donuts and trying to make healthier choices, but the next morning on her way into the office, Emma thought they all deserved donuts. She went through the drive-through of Mary Lou's and got herself a Peanut Butter Wonderful iced coffee, which was the most delicious thing ever, nut-flavored coffee with chocolate syrup. She only rarely indulged in those. She also ordered an assortment of donuts and Mickey's eyes lit up when she put the box down in the middle of the coffee table.

Her mother already knew what had happened the night before as Emma had called her as soon as Brady went home and assured her that she was okay. Emma told Mickey all the details of the night before and he was suitably impressed.

"Your father would have been proud, Emma. Good job recording the conversation."

Her mother congratulated her again but also looked concerned. "This can't ever happen again, Emma. If Brady hadn't been home, you could have been killed. We can't take chances like that. We have to be more careful in the future."

Emma knew she really meant that Emma needed to be more careful. "You're right. I know you're right, and I will be more careful. I promise. Did you hear anything from Rich?"

Her mother nodded. "Yes, I talked to him on the way in this morning and he said they have a pretty strong case now, thanks to your recording, and the FBI is still gathering more information. It looks like both Justin and Sheila are in a lot of trouble. But at least Justin didn't kill anyone."

"I still can't believe Sheila had Nancy killed," Emma said.

"It sounds like there was a lot of money involved. Rich said they researched her bank account and there were multiple payments of fifty thousand—every other month for the past year."

Mickey whistled. "That is a lot of money."

"And George had moved in with her. So, it was in his best interest to keep the money spigot flowing," her mother said.

"It's just so sad though," Emma said. "But Sheila didn't seem to regret it at all. She really didn't care about Nancy. Just the money."

"Well, I'm glad we were able to get some answers for Belinda and that Sheila and George will go to jail for a long time. I don't know about the two of you, but I'm looking forward to some less exciting cases. Workman's comp or insurance sound nice."

Emma had to agree. "I'm ready for something milder for sure. That was fun though…well, until the very end. It was a little nerve-racking," she admitted.

"And that won't happen again," her mother reminded her.

Emma smiled. "It won't."

They spent the rest of the morning working on a new skip-tracing case and were about to head to lunch when the main phone rang and Emma's mother answered. Mickey and Emma both eavesdropped on the conversation but it was hard to get a feel for what was being said on the other side.

"A cold case? You were a good friend of Fred's? Well, of course we'll meet with you. Tomorrow at ten am in our office is fine. We'll see you then, Kathryn."

Her mother hung up the phone and walked over to them, wearing a concerned look.

"Who was that?" Emma asked.

"She said her name was Kathryn Hughes and many years ago she was a good friend of your father's. It must have been after we divorced because her name wasn't familiar to me. She just moved back to Plymouth and wants our help with a cold case involving her sister. She said it's a long story and she'll explain it all to us tomorrow."

"Was her sister murdered?" Emma asked.

"I don't know. She didn't say. I hope not."

Mickey reached for another donut, blueberry-filled this time. "Well, I guess we'll find out tomorrow. Never a dull moment around here these days."

———

THANK YOU SO MUCH FOR READING PLYMOUTH Undercover! I hope you enjoyed the story. If you'd like to be notified when the next book in this series releases, please join my mailing list. Or sign up on my website, www.pamelakelley.com

If you enjoyed this story, you might also like my other two women's fiction mysteries, Trust and Motive.

Next up on June 8 is The Hotel, a women's fiction standalone novel set on Nantucket. Available everywhere —see an excerpt and all store links on my website.

I have a wonderful reader group on Facebook that you are welcome to join-two actually. My personal Pamela Kelley group is here. And I also started a mystery/thriller reader group with a few other authors that has lively discussions about what people are reading. You are very welcome to join one or both.